COLORING OUR WAY TO
CALAMITY

By
Richard Evans

"Civilizations die from suicide, not by murder"
Arnold J Toynbee, Historian

First Edition, December 2009

The characters, places and events depicted in this novel
are fictitious. Any similarity to actual persons, living
or dead, is purely coincidental.

Dedicated to all those who carry the scars
of the battle for school choice

I imagine you will pick up a
few more scars in the next
couple of years. They'll be
badges of honor

Good luck!

Richard Evans

CONTENTS

PART 1

THE CHOICE

PART 2

THE ALTERNATIVE

PART 1

THE CHOICE

CHAPTER 1
"The Empires of the future will be the Empires of the mind."
Winston Churchill, British Politician and Prime Minister

SEPTEMBER 2008

REYNOSA, MEXICO.

The machines in the plant had been turning all night. With each cycle, they hummed out the anthem of a changing world.

Outside, the sun was coming up and casting a yellowish glow on the cinder block walls of the little shacks with the corrugated roofs that were randomly scattered about what had, until quite recently, been a prairie. A maze of antennas testified to the astonishing capability of CNN to pervade third world communities well in advance of the development of a supply of potable running water. The TV screens inside the shacks sat on cardboard boxes. But they portrayed a vision of a distant, more desirable, existence. One worth working for, even though, at pay rates of less than two dollars per hour, it could take a while.

A warm breeze stirred the trash in the street while a couple of scrawny stray dogs began their day by copulating energetically on the trodden down earth trail that served as a sidewalk. They probably figured, correctly, that it would be far too hot later on.

The dubious ever-present aroma from the Rio Grande was masked, to some degree at least, by the thick black diesel fumes emanating from the tail pipes of hundreds of ancient half-size buses plying back and forth along the main thoroughfares. The combined effect of the sunrise, the humidity in the air, and the incomplete burning of fossil fuel was an acrid haze which permeated the growing city.

The destination of each bus, if indicated at all, was scrawled in white paint on the windows. Groups of waiting passengers mingled with school children in uniform among the sidewalk debris at unmarked stopping points along the way. Somehow they managed to identify which vehicle would transport them to the factories where they could launch their collective daily economic attack on an America that was showing little inclination to fight back.

SUNBURY, NEW HAMPSHIRE, UNITED STATES

While the Mexicans waited in the dawn, the school day was already in session in the Northeastern corner of the continent.

A comfortable mid-September sunshine was burning through the morning mist and drying out the dew which had lain heavily on the neat lawn adjacent to the public elementary school building in Sunbury. The principal, Duncan Markwell, surveyed the agreeable scene outside the window of the cozy office that was his sanctuary. The buses had arrived on time, and it would be a good day for holding PE classes outdoors, so all was well with the world. He was slim and fairly athletic himself, and often voiced concerns about youth obesity. More to the point though, PE used up lots of time and was very difficult for anyone to assess objectively.

It never would have occurred to him, but he occupied the front lines of America's only defense against the onslaught from the machines churning away beyond the nation's borders. To him, and others like him around the country, fell the responsibility of developing the national strategic reserve of intellectual capital. A capital that was the only asset the nation possessed that could possibly trigger sufficient innovation to build an economy capable of warding off low wage international competition.

In the classrooms that he supervised but rarely visited, down the corridors from his office, the emphasis was on building something else entirely. In the bright airy rooms, which each housed surprisingly few children and surprisingly many adults, the walls were covered with paintings that the students had undertaken. Bright gold stars and helpful teacher's guidance such as "Wow!" adorned each poster. A careful observer would have noted that many of the captions that the children had included in their drawings contained fundamental spelling mistakes. Often the mistakes were in close proximity to the "Wow!"s. But nobody seemed very concerned.

VILLA FLORIDA INDUSTRIAL PARK, REYNOSA, MEXICO

The plant where the bus dropped the Mexicans would have been a surprise to most residents of the United States.

Popular sentiment held that low wage foreign economic competition occurred exclusively in dirty, disease ridden old buildings that could be conveniently dismissed as "sweatshops". Belittling them thus made them sound inefficient and somehow less threatening. But as the Mexicans disgorged from the buses and headed for the workers' entrance, the reality was that a very different sort of workplace awaited them.

It was a brand new facility set on a large lot in one of several industrial parks that had sprung up on the outskirts of town. It covered an area the size of four or five football fields and provided employment, for the time being at least, for around three thousand local people.

A couple of dozen or more similar buildings, owned mainly by major United States corporations that were household names, dotted the surrounding landscape. Despite the fact that several more large steel frame shells were already under construction, there was clearly no shortage of available land. Brown and dry with an occasional scrub tree, the extent of the undeveloped tracts of the Villa Florida stretched on as far as the eye could penetrate the haze. Here and there, a malnourished cow or two could be made out grazing on the shriveled grass, blissfully unaware that global economic forces would shortly combine to force them into pastures new, or, more likely, some particularly unsavory local slaughter house.

The sun was already uncomfortably hot as the workers crossed the parking lot and passed through the swinging glass doors of the Mexican entrance. The twinge of the fierce air conditioning brought shivers and goose bumps to T-shirt clad torsos that had sweated against each other on the crowded buses just moments earlier.

Inside the building, the atmosphere was totally devoid of anything that suggested uplifting architecture, tradition or permanence. The interior resembled an aircraft hangar and function, not form, was plainly the operative by-word. There were no windows, but fluorescent tubes created twenty-four hour daylight. Work places were arranged in a rectangular grid like the streets of Manhattan. The place was spotlessly clean, almost sterile looking. A fresh coat of shiny gray paint covered the floor and fork lift trucks buzzed around the little highways marked out between the work centers.

There was a steady, but not overpowering, background noise. Production was occurring. Efficiently. Accurately. The Mexicans didn't fully understand it, but wealth was transferring, inexorably, in their direction with each completed piece that the fork lifts carted away.

A large SUV with Texas plates swung off the road and pulled up to the reserved parking in front of the executive entrance. Four white males, each distinctly portly in relation to the Mexicans, disembarked. They made a few jokes about the lingering effects of too much tequila from dinner the night before. The cost of the meal for the four of them had been far more than a month's wages for an assembly worker. The executives headed for the marble tiled main lobby and the comfortable, clean offices beyond.

SUNBURY, NEW HAMPSHIRE

In a public elementary school with an enrollment of five hundred children, most days there were one or two birthdays.

The principal had initiated the practice, years before, of students bringing in candy for their classmates on birthdays. It filled up quite a bit of time, and perpetuated the carefully constructed veneer of a caring atmosphere. It had become traditional that the celebrants would also visit his office for a while and bring him a sampling of the goodies.

On this day, being close to Halloween, a young man named Mike Southwick, from Miss Jones' first grade class, had brought some particularly appealing chocolates, shaped like pumpkins and covered in an orange icing.

Mike stayed and chatted while the principal chewed. He told Markwell that they had just put the bunny ears on today's cut and paste exercise with the hot glue gun and it needed a while to dry properly. He was sure he wasn't missing anything by tarrying in the office.

Mike closed the door behind him as he left. The principal grinned and shook his head. It was hard to discern if the expression on his face was kindly or supercilious. He had spent his entire career surrounding himself with an environment from which he could comfortably deflect all criticism. It wasn't too difficult really. Get his staff to write "A"'s on enough report cards and the parents hardly ever complained anyway. Then the superintendent stayed happy and the school board approved his annual raises. That was important to him, because the folks who ran the highly academic private school that his own sons attended kept bumping up the fees each year.

"Can't be helped," he thought to himself. "My kids need that sort of school."

REYNOSA, MEXICO

It was unsettling. Demeaning even. It hurt when foreign visitors to their country walked through the main door while the Mexicans, themselves, had to use a side entrance.

The Mexicans had heard the "gringos" tequila jokes many times.

But they understood that two economies were at work in Reynosa. The restaurants where the 'Norte Americanos' took their meals played no part in the life of the local people. Besides, another worry haunted the Mexicans.

The jobs had arrived along the US-Mexican border because of the NAFTA trade agreement signed by Presidents Clinton and Salinas in 1993. It permitted much freer movement of goods between the United States and Mexico. On many categories of materials, customs tariffs had been dismantled entirely. The so called Maquiladora regulations effectively made it much easier for Americans to establish businesses in Mexico to take advantage of the low labor rates prevalent there.

In the presidential debates prior to the US elections of 1992, Ross Perot had famously predicted a "giant sucking sound" of jobs moving to Mexico if NAFTA were signed.

He was right. The jobs went South in droves. But something else happened also. Americans learned how to make or buy material in large quantities from overseas. Not just oil and clothes, but washing machines, hair dryers and VCR's too.

As the goods poured in, a new paradigm appeared. American consumers' appetite for low cost stuff from abroad expanded exponentially. And so American business started to search for ways to obtain ever cheaper products for their voracious customers. NAFTA had taught them how to look.

There were already rumblings that the dramatic expansion of the Maquiladora trend was not as limitless as had once appeared. The Mexicans knew that wage rates in

Guatemala, India and a host of other places were even lower. And it wasn't just assembly labor that was affected. A good plant financial controller in India cost about a quarter of the wages that the same capabilities commanded in the United States.

It didn't take a genius to figure out that if the Americans had come to Mexico looking for cheap labor and factories with low overheads, then they would like what they were now seeing in India even better.

NAFTA had only just begun to bestow the blessings of an increasing prosperity on the border areas of Mexico. But already, it seemed, the first hints of the colder, harsher side of capitalism and competition were making themselves felt along the Rio Grande.

It has been said that Ted Turner's CNN cable news channel, and not Ronald Reagan's defiance, was the primary factor in the fall of the Berlin Wall. Reagan's speech writers conjured up stirring words to promote a more attractive societal structure than stagnating communism, but Turner was the better showman. Turner had pictures. And he had a method of delivering them to far more people than could hear or translate what Reagan was saying.

Communism was now all but dead on the planet, but CNN was still beaming out its images of the American good life. CNN's programming circled the globe, and the technological revolution had provided some sort of access to a TV to several billion people. The message had actually remained the same, but in a world that now had one dominant political culture instead of two competing ones, it was being received in a different way. No longer was its primary impact felt in rising political or ideological activity. What people overseas now read into what they saw on CNN was an enviable degree of materialism.

The Mexicans, just like the Chinese and the Indians, wanted the things that CNN had shown to them. It was inconceivable to them that commercial success could prove so fickle a mistress. Hadn't they put in the long hours in the boring jobs? Didn't they have a right to a more comfortable and prosperous future as a result? If the Maquiladora factories went elsewhere, who would clean up the mess and employ the hundreds of thousands of people who had flocked to the border region. They had no answers. All they could do was try to turn out more widgets every hour than the Chinese, and keep dumping the bi-products into the great river. For the time being, there were still more jobs than people. They could only wait, put up with the tequila jokes and the obscenely expensive dinners to which they were not invited, and hope for the best.

The machines kept turning and humming, turning and humming. An overwhelming torrent of wealth was in motion. There was no certainty that, in the future, this financial flood would continue to spread its blessings along the Rio Grande. But one thing was for sure; the flood was possessed of a fearsome current, and it was flowing away from the United States.

CHAPTER 2
"A rising tide of mediocrity that threatens our very future as a Nation"
Terrel Bell, Secretary of Education, 1983

SEPTEMBER 2008

SUNBURY, NEW HAMPSHIRE

Mike Southwick took his time getting back to his first grade classroom. Truth be told, the visit to the main office to take candy to the principal was about the most exciting thing that would happen to him that day. He knew that he wasn't missing anything vitally important by dawdling on his way back. In fact, it seemed to him, nothing critical had happened since school began a few weeks earlier. That puzzled him because he had expected the transition from Kindergarten to elementary school to involve quite a bit of hard work. He had concluded that it was just one of those things that he would probably understand better when he was a grown-up.

He had spent the previous school year at a nearby private kindergarten. His mother had taught him letter sounds from about age three, and the academic kindergarten had supported that effort so that the he was already quite a fluent reader of simple texts at the time that he entered first grade.

One of his favorite times of the day was when his Dad came home from work, sat him on a knee, and opened the Wall Street Journal in front of them. He had no idea what a "derivative" was, but, with an occasional assist could sound out that word and a lot of others as well. When he came to one that he couldn't manage, Dad would place his finger over all but the first part of the word and Mike would sound out the first syllable then the next, then the next, until he had the whole thing. The next time he saw the same word it would be easier. Sometimes Dad showed him how combinations of particular letters made surprising sounds that were different from the sounds of the letters themselves. Mike thought it was funny how that worked, but particularly liked learning those rules.

Many of the children who had been placed in the same first grade classroom as Mike, however, were not even at the point of identifying letters reliably. Although she would never publicly admit it, the huge spread of abilities in the class created a problem for the teacher.

Jenny Jones was twenty five years old, and starting her third year of teaching. Her own school career, although devoid of any signal academic achievement, had been documented by a series of highly complimentary report cards. All of her own teachers commented that she was a pleasure to have in class, and was someone who was very caring towards her peers. With her endeavors winning such a constant stream of approval, there had been little parental pressure placed on Jenny to spend her evenings studying. In fact, if she was really honest about it, she would be hard pressed to remember many days when she had carried a textbook home from school at all. Especially once she had a drivers' license, there were so many friends, and so many fascinating social activities to attend to. She seemed to be able to manage in class anyway.

Jenny's mother had been enormously proud of how well her daughter appeared to be progressing, and always spoke positively about the quality of the local schools and the great education that her daughter was obtaining. At every opportunity she would vote in full approval of new spending on facilities or staff contracts proposed by the school board. She never felt the need to actually look at the quality of the work that Jenny was producing, or even to check whether homework had been turned in on a regular basis. After all, the teachers all said it was marvelous, and she had a great deal of respect for them. In fact, she was of the opinion that it was important to give Jenny full responsibility for what she did in school. She thought there was at least a reasonable chance that her daughter might be headed to Harvard.

It had come as a major surprise to both Jenny and her family when she failed to crack a thousand combined in either of her two attempts at the SAT, and was denied admission to any of the name brand colleges to which she had confidently applied. There was a particular weakness on the Mathematics side where she had scored just above four hundred on each occasion. Her parents had thought that there must be a mistake and made an appointment to talk to the guidance counselor.

The counselor, who had held hundreds of such meetings in his thirty year career, had nodded his head and explained that, while the scores were in fact correct, things like this sometimes happened.

"Jenny may just not be a very good test taker, despite her high degree of intelligence which is indicated by the A grades she has been obtaining in Math for years." The parents felt better.

It was regrettable, he said, that some of the colleges had not been able to look beyond the test scores, which were, "Just one test on one day." But the outcome, he assured the parents, in no way reflected negatively on Jenny or the education she had received. Besides, she would obtain a "wonderful college experience" at Central New Hampshire State. "Had she considered teaching?"

The parents left. The guidance counselor shook his head. "The old 'high degree of intelligence' thing. Never fails," he thought.

So Jenny had headed off to teacher training, and graduated with a concentration in special education which the faculty at Central NH had assured her, correctly as it turned out, was the passport to employment in the teaching profession.

As well as being steered, by her advisor, towards Afro-centric elective courses such as "Black Lesbian Studies" and "The Truly Great Literature of Toni Morrison", her course load had featured a liberal emphasis that would have made the local ACLU chief blush.

As far as educational theory was concerned, a great deal of time and effort was expended at Central NH studying the thought of a cabal of educational authors whose theses appeared to rest on the assumption that any fact that could be looked up in a book should never be learned or memorized because it would occupy valuable brain cells that could otherwise be used for processing. Teachers, in this alternative view of the universe, exist solely to facilitate inquiry, not to deliver instruction.

Formal curriculum, so the theory goes, only serves to obstruct the natural process of student-directed discovery that the authors see as being the sole contributor to sound education.

There are several other central tenets to the philosophy.

The first is a sort of strange dichotomy that children are all different and so should be allowed to investigate whatever they each find interesting, yet are all the same and so can never be divided up along the lines of ability or motivation.

The second component, and the most assiduously pursued, is a steadfast opposition to any and all student testing. By removing objective measurement of capability, the only means of assessing the disastrous impact of trendy educational theories on the lives of other people's children is conveniently obliterated.

The last is that even those kids whose parents think that such an educational strategy is dangerous lunacy, should not be allowed to exercise an option to escape the cabal's vision for their school experience.

Such lack of choice creates a permanent job market for cabal followers. Teacher training schools, consequently, worship at this particular altar.

Shortly after taking up her teaching post in Sunbury, Jenny had been interviewed by the local newspaper for a piece that dealt with educational practices in the school district. She was asked about her thoughts regarding the direction that curriculum development should take.

By now, thoroughly indoctrinated in modern educational theory, and quite convinced that it had been the "old" way of thinking that had been the root cause of the disappointing outcome of her own school career, she answered confidently that her preference was that: "We should definitely de-emphasize the knowledge."

It was, then, into this atmosphere of complete denial of the very foundations of Western Civilization that Mike Southwick returned. He wasn't expecting much in the way of academics. He remembered that there was a new song to begin work on. It would take the entire time scheduled for Math for several days to learn the words well enough for the upcoming performance before the parents.

Nobody could argue that Jenny Jones was not a friendly and caring person. When the door opened and Mike walked in she beamed at him, walked over and put her hand protectively round his shoulders while guiding him back to his table.

"So," she said. "How was Mr. Markwell this morning."

Mike replied that the principal had seemed to be in a particularly cheerful mood. Mr. Markwell had shown him how he was preparing for the annual measurement of each student's health and fitness which was now required by the state. Unspoken had been the fact that in Markwell's view Math was expendable, but any opportunity to usurp a task that could arguably be regarded as parental responsibility must never be allowed to slip.

Two other students crawled past on all fours, pretending to be dogs. The "dogs" had been a fixture in the classroom all year.

"Woof," barked one.

"Woof, woof," replied the other.

"My goodness," said Jenny. "What a lot of barking today. What do you think dogs mean when they bark at each other?"

At Central NH she had been taught that the development of a future technological workforce required that she introduce scientific inquiry to the educational mix at every opportunity.

The canines clearly had no idea or interest in the answer to the question and headed off, still on all fours, in the opposite direction.

"Miss Jones?" asked Mike.

"Yes, dear."

"Why do they do that?"

Jenny Jones jumped at the opportunity to reinforce notions of tolerance that had been emphasized ad infinitum in her college program.

"Sometimes some people behave a little differently, that's all. It's very important that we don't judge them on that basis," she insisted.

Looking a little more stern than usual, Miss Jones proceeded to explain that the "dogs" suffered from a variety of unfortunate conditions that all had very long names.

Jenny Jones ushered Mike back to the table where he spent a large part of each day coloring. At Central NH it had been drilled into her over and over again that it would undermine the entire societal model to let some students advance academically when others were unable to.

A traditionalist, looking around the room might have concluded there were actually multiple different lessons going on at once. There were no rows of desks, and Miss Jones did not stand at the front of the class where every student could see her delivering instruction. Instead there were several tables around each of which sat four or five students. About one third of the students were positioned so as to be facing directly away from the blackboard. On the rare occasions when Jenny Jones tried to command the attention of the whole group simultaneously, these students had to do repeated pirouettes in order to write anything in their books.

As the "dogs" crawled around unrestrained, a variety of different things were happening at the tables. There were at least six children in the classroom who could not identify the letter "A", let alone any of the following ones in the alphabet.

It would have seemed reasonable, to anyone with any organizational sense at all, to cluster together all the children who couldn't identify "A" at one table, and teach them how to do that. And to put all the ones that could already read a little at another table and give them tasks that would advance their skills to the next level.

Extending the principle further, since there were several first grade classrooms, each constituted with the same student ability mix as Jenny Jones' room, it would have made still more sense to put all the students still working on identifying letters in one classroom. That way the teacher's entire time could have been devoted to teaching this important skill to those still in need of that instruction. In another room, another teacher could have been equally efficiently enhancing the reading of those with more highly developed capabilities.

But this common sense approach was quite definitely not welcome in the classrooms at Sunbury. In fact the exact opposite tactic was in place. The most advanced students were deliberately situated next to those that were struggling. The word "mentor" was heard a lot in staff meetings. The idea being, not that an adult would deliver valuable advice or instruction, but that one six year old would be able to explain how the world worked to another.

The most precious, and most expensive, resource of any school district is teacher time. By mixing the abilities in each classroom, and therefore deliberately diluting the amount of relevant instruction that could be delivered to each individual student, the school authorities, supported by the teachers' union, achieved one of their most cherished goals. They made the development of intellectual capital far more difficult than it needed to be.

At Sunbury, this surprising objective was augmented by the method employed to try to teach reading, which would also have come as quite a shock to your grandmother. The school district had implemented the hopeful sounding "Learning Through Discovery" program several years previously. One component of the program was the "Whole Language" reading method.

Fundamentally, Whole Language abandons the phonetic technique of de-coding words by sounding out vowels and consonants, in favor of having children look at pictures on the page and then attempt to guess what the words underneath might be. The method conveniently ignores the obvious question of what the children are supposed to do when there is no picture.

Despite its readily apparent shortcomings, Whole Language had its adamant defenders among teachers across the country. The reason had little to do with any effectiveness at advancing reading skills in young people. No, the reason for its enduring popularity amongst the suppliers of educational services was that it absolutely guaranteed a never-ending supply of eleven year olds who would could not read properly. All of them would need very expensive remedial services from the special education department. And, along with mixed ability classrooms which by definition require smaller class sizes, that meant jobs. Lots of jobs. And where there were jobs in schools there followed closely behind that most potent of all educational elixirs – union dues.

In short, the financial fortunes of the teachers' union were significantly improved if less children could read. The teachers in the United States formed the largest trade unions in the world. With all those members, and all those dues came power. Real power. By some estimates, seventy percent of the dues went for political purposes. It amounted to hundreds of millions of dollars each year. The loot was spread around federal and state legislators to try to make sure that nobody that mattered ever voted to dent that power by allowing competition from private providers for education funds, or by insisting that incredibly damaging ideas like mixed ability classes and whole language be outlawed. Power begat power. A never ending cycle. Perfect, for them.

Anyone, a concerned parent of an as yet illiterate third of fourth grader for example, who was prepared to stand up publicly and question the validity of Whole Language or the rationale behind mixed ability classrooms was therefore certain to get politically eviscerated by hordes of angry union members, indignant that anyone would have the nerve to threaten their turf. Letters from teachers would appear in the local newspaper about how the educators were insulted by the insinuation that what was happening in the classroom might not be "best practice". Decisions about teaching methods, they would say, "must be left to the professionals" who were fully versed in what the "latest research" had shown. Of course they were. They had written the research themselves.

Usually a brief onslaught was enough to convince even stout hearted parents that it was not in their interest to pursue the complaint. It also served to deter any other would be school critics, who often feared that retribution for their actions might be meted out on their children. Nobody wanted their kid assigned to being the back-end of the donkey in the school play.

So when Mike took his place at the tables, there wasn't a great deal of stimulating activity available to him.

The child sitting next to him was being instructed in how to hold a pencil by one of several adult "aides" in the classroom. He wasn't catching on too quickly.

"Miss Jones," said Mike. "What shall I do now? I finished all the worksheets before break."

"Good for you!" Said Jenny Jones.

She hated these moments. There were twenty-four students in her class. That meant, that in the approximately five hours per day that she had to manage the classroom, after subtractions for breaks, for lunch, and for PE, each child could expect to command about twelve minutes of her time.

She knew, she absolutely knew, because it had been drummed into her head at Central NH by every single education professor, that mixed ability classes represented best practice. But there was no denying that several times each day it crossed her mind that the approach was tricky to manage.

In addition to the dilution of the attention that she was able to give to each child, caused by the mingling of abilities in her classroom, there was also a greatly increased class preparation load. Were it the case that just about every child in the room were able to do the same sort of thing, she would still have had the considerable task of preparing twenty-five hours of lesson time each week. But, in effect, in order to provide relevant material to all twenty-four children she needed to prepare about a dozen different levels of lesson. It was a physical impossibility. Even with extensive evening and weekend time, there just weren't enough hours in the day. Coloring was the standard fallback.

"Well, what I would like you to do is some of your best coloring on this sheet," she handed the child an outline drawing of a mountain scene, with several varieties of animals in the foreground.

"But Miss Jones, I did that same picture yesterday. Perhaps I should write a story about the animals today? I could try doing that cursive handwriting that my Dad showed me. That was fun."

The child learning about pencil grips looked up with a wan look on his face. He was supposed to be mentored by Mike. One of the stated benefits of mixed ability classes was that all students would feel better about themselves if they were part of a diverse unit. But clearly, it was not going to help his self esteem one iota if his next door neighbor demonstrably started turning out voluminous literature, in cursive handwriting, while he was still forming letters.

Besides, if a child wrote a story, the parents expected it to be reviewed and commented on by the teacher, which meant a lot of work for Jenny Jones.

"Oh Mike. You shouldn't be trying cursive handwriting for at least a couple more years," Jenny told him. "Do the coloring. Yesterday some of the colors went over the lines, so I'd like you to try again, and this time be a little more careful." She comforted herself that this would work wonders for his fine motor skills. Actually the sloppiness of the day before had been caused by abject boredom.

She turned back to her other charges. There were four students in her class who owned "IEP's". Individual Education Plans were something Jenny had learned all about in college. They were possessed by every child diagnosed with a learning disability, and were commonly referred to as defining "special education."

When the original 'Individuals with Disabilities Education Act' (IDEA) that created IEP's had passed Congress in the nineteen-seventies, it was envisioned that in the worst, most blighted communities in the country, the numbers involved might reach ten percent of the population, but would be much lower everywhere else. IEP's stipulated all sorts of special conditions, services and environments that had to be maintained for special education students. Once an IEP was approved, it was almost never rescinded, and the school district, by law, had to support it whatever it said. That meant lots of legally mandated money, and lots more jobs.

Nobody objected to the arrangement where autism, for example, or sensory damage was involved. There was a general sense that whatever was necessary, to give those students the chance to do their best, was a justifiable expense. But not surprisingly, because there were no constraints placed on the number of IEP's that could be issued, the originally expected numbers were swamped in very short order. IDEA was, to all intents and purposes, a license to print money with which to hire more union employees.

A huge industry grew up around special education. In particular, a maze of medical diagnoses, often accompanied by the administration of potent medications, were applied to students exhibiting all manner of varieties of conduct.

Tens of thousands of educational specialists nationwide benefited financially from the reclassification of poor behavior as a medical disorder. And they lobbied hard politically to keep it that way, vilifying as a 'cruel Neanderthal' anyone seeking to impose restrictions on the sorts of conditions that should rightfully qualify for an IEP. They were not about to allow their gravy train to be derailed.

In wealthy, leafy Sunbury, hardly one of the anticipated high density IEP communities, the level of IEP students had been rising steadily, and had now reached almost twenty percent. With four IEP students out of twenty-four therefore, Jenny's classroom was somewhat under represented with IEP's. But dealing with those four students, who regularly behaved erratically but could not be disciplined under the terms of the IEP, took a large percentage of her classroom time, and further directed her attention away from the other students. Still, Jenny knew in her heart that she was doing the right thing. The other students would manage just fine investigating and studying by themselves.

One of the "dogs" burst into tears. Jenny rushed towards him.

As she passed, a student put his hand up and said, "Miss Jones, can you help me with this Math?"

But Jenny's eyes were fixed on the wailing "dog", no longer crawling around happily barking, but instead sitting on the floor with tears rolling down his face. There was a trickle of blood down his shin, and with grubby hands he was trying to pry out the thumb tack pin that had become embedded just below his left knee cap. To Jenny, he looked like a living, breathing law suit.

"Not now, honey," she said. Math would have to wait. Again.

CHAPTER 3

"It has been said that arguing against globalization is like arguing against the laws of gravity."

Kofi Annan, former Secretary General of the United Nations

SEPTEMBER 2008

SHOPPING PLAZA, NEW HAMPSHIRE

Beth Southwick pushed the stroller that held Mike's younger sister through the swing doors of the massive box of a building which housed one branch of a giant retail chain.

"How do you get to be the world's biggest and best at anything," she pondered. "If the outer limit of your employees' creativity is architecture like this?"

The familiar stale aroma of cheap plastic and popcorn assailed her senses. Her mother hated the place.

"Beth, dear," she would lecture. "Why don't you buy the children's clothes at Filene's?"

It had been easier in mother's time. The expected trappings of middle class status were nowhere near as extensive. In those days you could still be perceived to be comfortably off if the family owned just one car and the kids played with a bat and ball outdoors in the yard all summer.

The perception was what counted. For Beth's family it took a large house, two quality cars, spring breaks in the islands and a host of other expenses to maintain the image of effortless economic success which meant so much in her social circle. It all cost a lot.

Still, nobody could see if your underwear came from a discounter. So a couple of times a month, Beth would push a cart around the aisles and load up on things that could be put away in drawers and cupboards out of the neighbors' field of view. It saved a ton of money which helped with the credit card bills that always seemed to be getting larger, and only her mother ever got to know.

The store held a staggering variety of merchandise. Clothes from Indonesia, power tools from China, computer cables from Mexico.

"Dear God, can't we make anything in America, these days?" she thought, throwing some notepads that bore the "Made in Pakistan" moniker into the cart.

It was an issue that had hovered around the edges of her consciousness for some years. More recently though, events had combined to force a more serious consideration of the question. The subject made her uncomfortable, but the more she tried to push it away the more it intruded on her psyche.

14

There was the family down the road. It had seemed as though the man of the house had a pretty good job. He was driving around in an Audi. But then he started being seen around the neighborhood during the week, and the whispering began that his job had been "outsourced". Then they moved away to somewhere in the back of beyond in the Carolinas that sounded really awful. The house had been sold in a hurry at a price that had irritated Beth because it set a precedent for her neighborhood that she considered far too cheap.

Beth Southwick was not an unintelligent person. She held a university degree, and had occupied a decent job in a local PR firm before the kids had arrived. She wanted to stay at home with them and be involved with their time in school. Her older son had just entered first grade. The little one would go to pre-school in a year's time. So she had left the PR job. It made things difficult for the family financially. Between the two mortgages, the two car loans and the credit cards, they had what seemed to her like an enormous amount of debt.

Smart as she was, the conflicting messages in the press and on TV about the impact of what everyone called a "global economy" worried and confused her. For every commentator who said that there wouldn't be any jobs left in America, there was another who said that the benefit of being able to buy lots of cheap stuff more than made up for that. She tossed a five dollar bonus pack of a dozen pairs of short socks, "Made in Thailand", into the cart. She didn't know who to believe.

She remembered the previous presidential election. The two Democratic Senators, Kerry and Edwards who had challenged incumbent George W. Bush had grasped the issue like bulldogs, and wouldn't let go. They repeatedly blamed Bush for every manufacturing job that had been lost in America for the previous four years. Kerry had been a supporter of NAFTA when Democratic President Clinton had signed it. But "greedy" and "insensitive" seemed to be the labels Kerry now sought to attach to any business CEO who took advantage of the new regulations which his vote had helped to create.

She had an uneasy feeling that it wasn't just the quantity of jobs that was at issue, but the quality. Rumor in the neighborhood was that the poor fellow who had sold his house and moved away ended up taking a fifty percent pay cut. She shuddered when she thought about what that degree of lost income could do to her family budget.

Her husband, Douglas, was a financial executive with an auto parts manufacturer. Recently, work had not been much fun at all. Even his company was now making some components in a plant in Malaysia and there was always pressure to reduce overhead costs. Some middle managers had been let go and Douglas was always telling her about a lot of whispered conversations behind closed doors at the office.

Beth spent a lot more time, now, wondering about where this might all lead for her children. Would she and Douglas be able to provide opportunities for a good life for them? Would she have to go back to work? What sort of job might await her if she did?

Her protective motherly instincts led her to one certain conclusion. The world seemed to be heading ever more in the direction of survival of the fittest and there didn't seem to be one thing that any of the politicians could actually do about that despite all their bluster and claims. The definition of "fittest" seemed no longer to mean "strongest", it meant "smartest". The number of jobs in America like the one that Douglas held down was going to be reduced, but the number of people wanting them was going to increase. There was only one solution: position her own children so that they could elbow their way to the front of the line.

She passed through the checkout, adding another hundred dollars to the mountain of debt on the credit card, and headed for the exit. Outside, a fairly well dressed man stood facing the exit with a sign that said: "Please help – will work for food." She hurried past.

"God, it's like the Third World," she thought.

What on earth would become of America? Beth had never actually been to a third world country, but it didn't look all that great on TV.

As she crossed the parking lot in the fresh crisp Autumn air, she decided she needed to know a bit more about how all of this globalization fit together and what it meant to her family. A trip to the local library was in order.

CHAPTER 4

"Our future is not in competing at the low-level wage job; it is in creating high-wage, new technology jobs based on our skills and our productivity."
John Kerry, United States Senator

SEPTEMBER 2008

SUNBURY, NEW HAMPSHIRE

She sat on her porch mulling it all over.

She had read about the British historian Toynbee, who had observed that: "Civilizations die from suicide, not by murder." That's what seemed, to her at least, to be happening to America.

It wasn't as if there was a lack of warning. It was, after all, a long time ago that all the clothes began carrying "Made in Hong Kong" labels.

There was a reason, she now understood, why the clothes manufacturing had gone offshore first. They were easy to make. There isn't much of a financial entry barrier to setting up a clothing factory. Just cut down some trees in the jungle, put up a canopy in the clearing, buy a few sewing machines, and hey presto – you're a profitable supplier of huge quantities of jeans to American retailers. Clothes have a fairly large labor content relative to other commodities of similar cost, so the percentage gain on the overall product cost to be achieved by using employees who only get paid five dollars a day, if they are lucky, is substantial.

She had browsed through Adam Smith's seminal work on economics, "The Wealth of Nations". Writing around the time of the American revolution, the canny old Scot had foreseen precisely what was going to happen. Smith's premise was simple: firstly, all trade must be good for both parties or they would not undertake the deal. Therefore the more trade occurs the better off everyone becomes. Secondly, if a society pursues free trade, it had better watch out because the money and the jobs will eventually flow to the most efficient providers.

Focusing on what it took to become one of these efficient providers, Smith had been the first to formally define the advantages of the division of labor. His famous example described how an artisan attempting to make pins could probably only produce ten or twenty pins a day if, all by himself, he had to cut and polish the shaft of the pin, shape the head and then glue the two together. But if there were several artisans, each becoming expert at one particular element of the task, then, between them, they might produce thousands of pins in a day, raising their combined productivity to ten or even a hundred times the level of a sole practitioner.

From pin-cutting artisans, to the textile mills of the industrial revolution, to Henry Ford's production lines, and finally to the global supply chains of the twenty-first century, Smith's followers had set in motion a never ending continuum of improvement in productivity. Marching lockstep with mankind's ever growing ability to produce – in fact driving that ability - was mankind's ever growing desire

17

for manufactured creature comforts. Abigail Adams used to send her husband off on his historic trips to Europe with shopping lists that featured prominently the very pins that Smith was describing how to manufacture. After that, we all wanted nice clothes from the textile mills, one of Henry's Model-T's and, more recently, cheap TV's from China.

Each new technology that came along folded rapidly into the surge of supply and demand. Water power first drove the mills along the Merrimack river, later electricity did a better and more reliable job. Of late, the fax machines and then the internet had allowed information about worldwide demand to be disseminated to all corners of the globe at rates that even Adam Smith could have never imagined. Boeing 747's and container ships sent ever increasing quantities of manufactured goods back in the other direction in response to voracious consumers.

What had become known as "globalization" was nothing more or less than Smith's division of labor – on steroids.

The overall result was pretty much exactly what Smith's crystal ball had revealed to him. He had been the first to realize that how "well off" a particular nation was did not depend on the amount of gold it had in a vault. You couldn't eat that after all. It depended on the amount of stuff that you made, and were able to trade for other stuff that you wanted. In the passing of just a couple of hundred summers, a blink of the eye in human history, large parts of humanity used the blessings of expanded trade to emerge from the filth, discomfort and disease which, previously, only the Romans had even attempted to hold at bay. And it felt good.

As far as Americans were concerned there was only one catch.

After the Second World War, it was pretty much a case of "last man standing". The United States, rich in natural resources, neither physically scarred by the conflict, like Europe and Japan, nor fettered by a repressive social order, like Russia, was ideally placed to convert its advantages into unprecedented economic prosperity for its citizens. It did so with an enthusiasm and energy unmatched in human history. There was a lot of hard work involved, but nevertheless, the second half of the twentieth century was a cakewalk for anyone fortunate enough to find domicile in America.

But recently it had all started to unravel.

Some commentators, like Thomas Friedman for example, believed it was the laying of all the fiber optic networks under the sea that heralded the seismic economic upheaval that happened next. He wrote in his "The World is Flat", that expanding the internet had allowed several billion people, who had previously been geographically isolated from the economic boom, to "march on to the playing field".

Whether it was that or something else, the undeniable truth was that a whole bunch of folks around the planet had not only seen the good times rolling on TV, they were also now in a position to get a piece of the action.

The two things that most of these folks had in common were that they were willing to work for the equivalent of a few bucks a day, and they had never even heard of health insurance.

At first, in the seventies and eighties, the use of cheap overseas labor was not at all a bad deal for Americans. It enabled them to buy basic commodities, particularly clothes, more cheaply in the stores. The people in some small company towns in the South got clobbered when the sewing rooms closed down, but the overall number of job losses was not so great that other sectors of the economy, notably service industries, couldn't pick up the slack in semi-skilled labor.

Any heavy duty, skilled manufacturing, or white collar occupation, was protected by geography and by the expense and difficulty of setting up overseas facilities. You couldn't put a car plant under that same canopy in the jungle that was making jeans; there wasn't anybody around to program the robots for one thing. So the US auto workers were just fine, and felt secure enough in their jobs to keep demanding extraordinarily large increases in wages and benefits. Ford and General Motors started to spend more on health care for their employees than they did on steel for their products.

But as time went on, more and more products, which had once been regarded as strictly "Made in America", because nobody else had the financial or intellectual resources to start the plants, or the access to the markets to sell into, began to appear in the containers arriving in America's ports.

The rest of the world was travelling up the economic curve. The model was simple and predictable. Make some money stitching up clothes, then start looking around for other, more profitable, product lines to supply. Invest the proceeds from the previous efforts, and become a major supplier in the next one.

First it was the clothes and plastic knick knacks, then it was the domestic appliances, then the cars. And it didn't stop there. The internet just super-charged the rate of change. Anything that could be digitized suddenly became a target. Software could be maintained in Bangalore with the added advantage that the time difference enabled problems to be fixed while Americans were asleep. An executive in New York, struggling to get information one evening from the corporate computers, could arrive at work the next morning to find the report that he needed sitting neatly on his desk. Even paralegals in law offices discovered that they weren't safe because briefs could be sent instantaneously to Asia where competent legal research into American law could be performed at a fraction of the cost of having the same work done in America.

Of course, with each new group of products that was manufactured overseas, a new group of Americans found themselves without the jobs that had provided their livelihood. They had to find something else to do and hope that it would generate sufficient income to preserve their standard of living.

There was a limit, though, to the amount of slack that could be taken up. And a limit to the number of jobs of equal compensation that existed in the US economy. For

19

many people, most of all those without highly developed skills, the "off-shoring" of their jobs meant serious economic hardship.

Many did not even realize what had happened to them. They complained that they were victims of greedy CEO's who cared only about profits, not people.

The reality was that they were victims all right – but it wasn't the CEO's fault. After all, if you are the CEO of a company that makes widgets, and all of a sudden your competitor starts bringing the things in from Korea for half the cost at which you can make them, what are you supposed to do? If you soldier on with expensive domestic manufacturing, all your customers start buying from your competitor and you end up having to close your doors and throw everyone, not just your manufacturing employees, out on the street. Hardly a recipe for "caring".

No, what had done in these unfortunate folks was not a lack of CEO "caring" – it was capitalism.

Beth paused in her musings, and sipped at the coffee in the old mug. The day was bright and sunny, one of those New England Fall mornings to die for. There was a crispness in the air and the shade on the porch was cool enough that she pulled her cardigan closer around her shoulders. On the adjacent lawn, the first dead leaves were dropping on to the warm sunlit grass. "Some things the Chinese can't have", she thought.

Then she chuckled. Even that was not necessarily true. She remembered how shocked she had been a few weeks earlier when the Belgian giant beverage company InBev had acquired Anheuser Busch. She didn't even drink beer, but the notion that an American icon brand like Bud could belong to a company from another country had been deeply disturbing to her. How could that happen?

As she had read on she had learned that world economics was not as complicated a subject as it seemed. There were just a lot of fancy financial vehicles and transactions around that made a fairly simple concept appear complex. In plain terms, by 2008, the US trade deficit was running at about two billion dollars per day! The trade deficit is the name given to the difference between the value of exports and imports. In other words Americans were buying two billion dollars more per day from all overseas countries combined, than we were selling to them. That is known as a trade imbalance. Divided equally amongst everyone in the US, it came to almost a thousand dollars each month for a family of four. That seemed like an awful lot. It was almost as much as Beth's mortgage payment.

We buy goods from the other countries with our money – dollars. (Or we can buy it with their currency, but then we have to buy their currency first with our dollars, so it's the same thing). If they don't want any of the goods that we make, and apparently in 2008 that was the case to the tune of two billion per day, then they end up sitting on a huge pile of US dollars.

But you can't use US dollars in a supermarket in Shanghai, and even if you could, the supermarket owner would just end up sitting on the pile of dollars instead of his customer. So, sooner or later those dollars have to come back to America, and when they do, the new owner of the dollars wants something of equivalent value in return. What are his options if he doesn't want any of our raw materials or consumable goods that we manufacture? It's quite simple – he has to buy assets instead. So he selects from a smorgasbord of American baubles. He can buy stock in our companies – or purchase control of the whole damn thing if he wants, as was the case with Anheuser Busch. He can buy golf courses, or skyscrapers, ranch land, municipal bonds or federal debt. Or he can deposit it in an American bank and draw interest on it.

The net effect is that the United States brings in an assortment of products that we consume, and in return, because people in other countries don't want as many of our products as we want of theirs, they get to own a whole bunch of things that we previously thought of as being as American as apple pie.

By 2008, in addition to all the trade deficits, the United States government had racked up a debt of about ten trillion dollars. That came to about one hundred and twenty thousand dollars for each family of four. More than half of that debt was held by overseas investors. It was inevitable that sooner or later the investors were going to want a seat at the table where decisions impacting their investment were made.

For every dollar of trade imbalance and government debt held overseas we were giving up some ownership of America.

She put down the coffee cup. Maybe the Chinese would, after all, soon be telling her how and where she could enjoy Fall mornings like the one that was before her now.

It was ironic really, she thought. The three central tenets of capitalism were: The rule of law, private property, and free markets. America had endorsed all three, and reaped the blessings of this social system in the twentieth century. The wealth and prosperity it had created had propelled the nation to the degree that the period was known as "The American Century". Wealth had translated into power, and America had overwhelmed both Fascism and Communism, and made a pretty good dent in the scourge of terrorism.

After all that, she chuckled to herself, we had succumbed to our inability to recognize and meet the demands placed on us by capitalism. It would go down, she thought, as one of the ultimate own goals in all of recorded history.

It wasn't that capitalism was wrong. It had provided, and continued to provide, the direction and the means for humankind to live in a level of comfort never experienced before. What America had failed to notice, however, was that capitalism didn't play favorites. Like all the great Empires and powers of history, America had assumed that the gravy train would roll on forever with Americans, this time, sitting pretty as capitalism's "chosen ones".

It was not to be.

The British had shown the world how to play cricket, not for one moment thinking that a bunch of descendants of their slaves might figure out a better way to do it.

Now, the same thing had happened to America in the world of business. All sorts of folks around the planet had suddenly discovered how to use mass production to make things far less expensively than we could. More importantly they had also figured out that America was the largest marketplace in the world, and was also politically committed to using free trade as the vehicle for spreading its creed of individual freedom.

The United States was not going to keep the goods of another country out of their marketplace just because those goods were cheap. Quite the opposite in fact. The country was covered in these things called Walmarts.

And you could hardly get bombed for making cheap TV's. The worm had turned.

It was capitalism, not greedy CEO's that had not been "caring", and had displaced workers. Not that there was any better system of social organization in view. The alternative, a planned economy that collectivized all costs and benefits, had proved responsible for more human misery than any other economic model wherever, and whenever, it had been tried in the world.

What had really happened was that the communications revolution had brought a colossal influx of new players into the global economy. The vast majority of them provided unskilled, or at best semi-skilled, labor.

The laws of supply and demand had then woven their unavoidable pattern. With a worldwide glut of that type of labor, the price of an hour of manual work predictably went through the floorboards. There were literally billions of people willing to exchange a day of labor for a few dollars. And now, with communications and transportation technology providing the means to access that pool, the fall in the price of goods that required semi-skilled labor, or less, to manufacture was inevitable.

American workers had quite simply priced themselves out of the market in the manufacture of goods that had, for so long, generated a comfortable lifestyle for the country. American consumers were not willing to pay the prices of goods that were manufactured using employees who earned thirty dollars an hour and demanded a health plan.

And there was the essence of the problem. Capitalism was marvelous, but it wasn't static. Societies that signed up committed themselves to an ongoing march up the tree of prosperity from clothes to appliances to cars, to high technology. You had to move or die.

What had happened to America was that, fat and happy, it had not put in the sweat equity that it needed to acquire the workforce required for the next step. The lifestyle it took for granted as a birthright could no longer be provided by the diminishing wealth generation of assembly line style production. Competition, and the resulting lowering of prices, meant that those days would never return. There was still money to be made for sure, but increasingly it was going to take a post-industrial caliber workforce to make that wealth materialize.

The sad truth was that set against this undeniable, and desperate, need for a workforce with much higher skill levels, the United States was graduating five million kids a year from the public schools. Less than half of them could crack a thousand combined on the SAT test.

All of Beth's study had brought her to one startling conclusion. Although times had occasionally seemed tough in her lifetime, she had actually lived the highlight reel of America's period in history's sun. Things were going to be an awful lot tougher for her children.

And who would speak for them?

She rose from her seat on the porch and walked inside the house. On the wall in the small hallway was a large wooden picture frame, divided up into multiple apertures surrounding a small central mirror. The frame was filled with a half dozen pictures of her family taken on vacation a couple of years previously. Staring back at her, from the mirror in the center, was the answer to her question.

Much later she would look back on this moment as a turning point in her life.

She had always been uncomfortable in any sort of spotlight. At school she had never auditioned for the school play, or made announcements about events during assembly.

That fear remained. But, now, rising up next to it was another, perhaps even greater, anxiety. The concern that if nothing changed, her children's future was looking decidedly bleak.

She didn't yet know what she was going to do, or what she might be able to accomplish. But she had arrived at the point which is the beginning of many careers in the public square. The moment when the discomfort associated with standing up and speaking your mind in public finally becomes less than the frustration of accepting the results of the status quo.

Sitting on her porch that morning, she had crossed her personal Rubicon. And, just like Julius Caesar in another era, from that point on there could be no going back.

CHAPTER 5
"We must not confuse dissent with disloyalty."
Edward R Murrow, Broadcast Journalist

SEPTEMBER 2008

SUNBURY BAGEL SHOP, SUNBURY, NEW HAMPSHIRE

It had all begun innocently enough with an invitation to a meeting with a few of the other mothers who had kids in the same first grade class.

"Wouldn't it be nice," said the voice on the other end of the phone. "Since our kids are going to be in the same class, if we all got together early in the school year."

The chosen venue was the local Sunbury Bagel Shop. Half a dozen moms would eventually show up.

The mothers straggled in with the usual assortment of other infants and the associated paraphernalia of carriages and removable car seats.

After an exchange of the usual litany of complaints about the impossibility of the task of keeping everything together in the hurly burly world of children's activities that had engulfed the nation, the discussion had turned to the thing that they had most in common: the local school system.

Sunbury was situated in southwest New Hampshire. A bedroom community of around twenty thousand residents, it was known for its pleasant surroundings and well regarded public school system. The sky high property taxes that resulted from rapidly increasing school district budgets had not deterred families from relocating into the area. Beth's family was one of them. The lure of a safe and clean learning environment for children created a buoyant real estate market. By day, many of the town's local officials were also involved in the real estate business. At the evening meetings of their public committees and boards, the same officials aggressively pursued new public building projects as an added incentive to attract prospective clients to their private real estate companies.

The waitress delivered the coffee and bagels and the conversation began in earnest. There was a noticeable social pecking order amongst those present, Beth observed. Seniority seemed to depend not only on personal wealth, but also on the degree of involvement in volunteer activities in the public schools. Pam Jackson was a large woman with a loud voice who was one of Beth's neighbors. As such she didn't live in one of the town's trophy homes, but Pam had recently been elected chair of the PTA and wasn't about to let anybody forget the fact.

Her daughter, beginning fourth grade, was the oldest of the offspring of the assembled group. It was her younger child who was in the same class as Beth's son. Pam referred to the principal and other administrators of the school by their first names, suggesting an easy familiarity which struck a rather false chord with Beth.

"I was just telling Duncan the other day," she held forth, referring to the school principal. "How lucky we are in Sunbury to have such a wonderful school system. The PTA works so well together in organizing all the events. The concert is going to be just marvelous. Every class is working so hard on their songs. There's a bake sale in the lobby that evening by the way. Who can make brownies?"

Beth looked around the group and thought she perceived a subtle undercurrent of division. Joanie Wesson was gazing at Pam with a barely concealed admiration and nodding at every point.

"She just cannot wait for her turn at that PTA job," thought Beth.

Beth hadn't known Joanie previously, but she was already getting an impression that they might not grow to be best friends. Joanie's attire did not speak to a particular degree of prosperity, and Beth guessed, correctly as it turned out, that she probably saw a significant role in the PTA as her only opportunity to be somebody in Sunbury.

"Brownies aren't my specialty, but I could bring cookies," chimed in Jan Clovis.

"OK, you're committed now, though. You're in my book," responded Pam smiling and scribbling on a notepad.

Joanie laughed, a trifle too hysterically in Beth's opinion, and made sure that her name also went in the book for the brownies.

Beth sensed, though, that Chloe Roberts and particularly Ying Chang seemed less enthusiastic.

The conversation meandered on through two refills of the coffee cups. This was really break time for mothers whose heavy duty shift began later in the day with taxi service to soccer games, ballet lessons, doctors, dentists and band practice.

Pam held forth, with her superior knowledge, on the inner workings of the schools. It was vitally important she pontificated, loudly enough that the entire restaurant could hear, for everyone to get behind the school board's proposal for a new school which would be voted on the following spring. She was on first name terms with the board members as well, and had been recruited by them to organize "coffees" all over town over the next few months to meet with residents to promote the project. There had been some opposition from taxpayer groups.

"Some people just don't understand – and they never will," Pam complained. "Our children need a good education."

Pam sallied on under full, unstoppable sail. The list of names dropped, the catalog of events planned, and the accolades for the local schools turned into a blur for Beth. Her mind wandered to an op-ed article she had read in the Sunbury News written a couple of weeks earlier by one of Pam's opponents in the taxpayer group. The article had pointed out that the budget for the local schools amounted to almost $13,000 for every student served. As Sunbury expanded, not only did the overall budget increase, but the cost per student was increasing as well. There didn't seem to be any economy of scale.

The article asked an economic question. Instead of continuing to expand the public schools with new buildings to meet the ever increasing demand, might it be a better idea to offer some residents a financial incentive to explore other educational settings for their children? Specifically, the question posed was whether the school board's building proposal, which was based on an expectation of steadily increasing school population, was necessary at all if just enough students were offered this incentive so that the population of the public schools stopped growing and remained the same.

The article suggested that a "voucher", a direct payment of around $3,000 or $4,000 that could only be used to pay tuition at a private school, might achieve this effect. It was certainly a lot less than the $13,000 per student cost of expanding the public system. The writer also asked whether the educational outcome might even be stronger, and whether the element of competition introduced might positively impact the performance of the public schools.

The piece had drawn an immediate and fierce response in the "Letters to the Editor" section of the very next edition. One Jim Mortensen, who Beth discovered for the first time was chairman of the school board, castigated the article and accused the author of "divisiveness" and an ongoing agenda to "destroy public education". Joan Simons, president of the Sunbury Education Association which was the local chapter of the teachers' union, had expressed similar sentiment. Ms. Simons was also outraged that anyone might suggest that the schools' performance needed any improvement. She had taught in Sunbury for thirty-one years, her letter said, and in that time had never observed anything other than standards which represented the absolute pinnacle of her profession. She concluded with an appeal to residents to oppose any "draining of funds from the local public schools at a time when they are so desperately needed."

Beth had immediately noticed the parallel between the concept of the voucher and the outsourcing of business that her husband had been so concerned about of late. It was far cheaper for Douglas' firm to buy new parts that they needed from overseas than to expand their own factory and build the parts themselves using union wage rates and benefits. The factory wasn't in decline, and none of the shop floor labor had been let go. It just wasn't growing anymore the way it had done before. If the concept made sense for business didn't it also make sense for schools? Why were the local officials so incensed about the idea?

The private school element of the idea also appealed to her. In her mind, "private" had a connotation of quality that, if she were brutally honest with herself, she hadn't really seen in the Sunbury public system.

There were a couple of private schools in the vicinity of Sunbury. One was the Catholic St. Jude's and the other was an academy in the neighboring town of Chertsey. Fees at St. Jude's were about $4,500 per year, and perhaps twice that much at the academy. Beth wondered why it cost $13,000 for every student that attended the public schools.

Beth had seen the St. Jude's kids in their uniforms and thought it looked quite a lot more business like than the Sunbury public schools. But she wasn't sure if she wanted a Catholic education for her family despite all the stories of first graders writing book reports. She wasn't opposed to religion, but as a non-participant herself she felt mildly uneasy about putting her kids in classrooms where everyone was crossing themselves all the time.

Chertsey was a different story. They had a uniform too, and parents that she had spoken with related tales of a keenly academic environment. She would love to see her children in such a place. With her family's present financial situation, though, Chertsey's fees were out of the question. But if she worked part time and was able to obtain one of these "vouchers", it would effectively become much cheaper and maybe they could swing it.

Pam was still dominating the conversation with her accounts of the people and personalities of the school system. About every other word was "marvelous" or "wonderful". Jan and Joanie hung on every syllable, but Chloe and Ying were beginning to appear a bit bored. Chloe glanced at her watch.

Beth tried her best to fix an attentive look on her face and drifted back to her private reverie about Sunbury Elementary. She had been full of optimism when Mike had begun there a few weeks earlier. After everything the real estate agent had told them about the school district, it seemed fairly certain that most kids there would put Einstein to shame by the time they reached third grade. It hadn't taken her long, though, to notice that huge amounts of time seemed to pass without anything very tangible happening.

The teacher was certainly friendly enough. The classroom was clean and colorful, and Mike was quite happy there. But it was impossible to deny that there were not many days when he came home with anything more than pages and pages of coloring. Cut and paste, too, was a favorite activity. When she had volunteered to help out for a couple of days in the classroom, ostensibly out of civic duty but really to get a first hand look at what was going on, she had been assigned to cut up green plastic bags that would turn into leaves on the cut and paste Christmas tree.

It wasn't easy and she had borne the bruise from the scissors on her thumb for several days. Another scar had lasted longer though. That was the distinct impression she had received that the activities in the classroom, while pleasant and non-threatening, didn't bear much resemblance to her definition of "a good education". In fact, to be absolutely truthful, it looked like a complete waste of time.

In particular, she had been shocked by something called "exploring time". For almost an hour the children had been free to roam unsupervised around the classroom stopping at different "laboratories" to conduct their own learning. The laboratories were tables or little stands covered with all sorts of supposed learning aids. There was one for science, another for Math and, of course, a particularly well equipped and popular one for art. While the kids had roamed, the teacher had sat next to Beth, who was still cutting, and explained that the purpose of "exploring time" was to allow the children to exercise their creativity in building their own educational program.

Since, in Beth's experience, Mike needed about ten direct instructions just to get dressed in the morning she had a difficult time envisioning this accomplishment. But she had smiled and kept her thoughts to herself.

She was aware that some parents thought it best not to complain publicly about the schools. She had heard that kids could then be singled out for classes with the least effective teachers, not given parts in the school play or opportunities on the sports teams. In particular, she sensed there was some degree of social ostracizing of any parent who wasn't thought of as a team player for the public schools. She certainly wouldn't want her name in print on the receiving end of letters such as the ones written about the op-ed author.

Perhaps, though, an informal meeting like this, away from the school itself, was an appropriate place to bring up her concerns.

Pam, her inventory of superlatives temporarily exhausted, had paused to draw breath. Chloe and Ying looked as if they were going to seize the opportunity for escape and were fumbling to pick up their belongings.

"But what about the test scores?" Beth blurted out.

Five pairs of eyes turned on her with various degrees of surprise, interest and, in one case, rising suspicion. Chloe released the hold on her bag. Ying looked suddenly less indifferent. Beth felt her face flush slightly. She hadn't really meant it to sound like that, but she knew that if she didn't get straight to the point Pam would just monopolize the discussion again and she'd never get to say what was on her mind.

"What about them?" asked Pam with a tone very different from the one she had employed for the past half hour.

The State of New Hampshire administered standardized tests every year to all children in third, eighth and eleventh grade public education. The results were published in the newspapers. Beth had been astonished to learn that, in common with many other communities in the state, only about a third of the eleventh grade students at Sunbury were able to register a score of "Proficient" in Math. Hardly any had achieved the higher grade of "Proficient with Distinction". Apparently, in addition to testing Math, English and Science, the state also used to examine social studies. The results statewide, in that area, had been abysmal. Under advice from teaching professionals who considered that the social studies exam relied too much on rote learning of facts like the approximate date of the American Revolution and the two sides in the Civil War, the subject had recently been quietly discontinued.

"Well," started Beth. "I was just a little surprised that with everything we're told about how well our schools are working, that more of the kids aren't getting better scores."

"Oh, that's just one test on one day. They're all doing really well. That test doesn't prove much," insisted Pam who was already wearing an expression midway between irritation and frustration. Dissent was not welcome. Beth had already crossed that line and was now permanently marked as someone to be watched very carefully. Perhaps even as an enemy.

Beth wondered whether Pam had a page in her book for listing dangerous opponents.

"I don't really believe in standardized tests, anyway," agreed Joanie. "It seems very arbitrary. I think a more holistic approach is better. What if you're not a good test taker?"

The teacher had used the word "holistic" while explaining "exploring time". Beth had no clue what it meant and was certain that Joanie didn't either. But it sounded deep.

Chloe and Ying were looking at her, paying far more attention than a couple of minutes earlier, but not giving much visible indication of support either. Beth decided to go one more round on her own.

"I know that the results were close to the state average, but I was expecting that in a town like this, where we don't have too much in the way of poverty or social problems, the results might actually be quite a bit better than average. I just wonder whether we're making it difficult enough in class to get the best out of our kids."

"You can test kids to death," Pam pronounced. "I just think we have to leave it up to the professionals to decide what's best."

"But isn't leaving it up to them what we've been doing that's produced these results?" Beth persisted, remembering the confidence that had exuded from the teacher, Miss Jones, who had explained "exploring time". She was no longer at all certain that she wanted to leave everything up to them.

"Well," said Pam, who plainly was not accustomed to having her opinion challenged on the subject at hand. "I suppose if you don't like it you can always send your children to private school. Anyway, I have to go"

The meeting had apparently come to an awkward end and the participants returned to neutral corners. Pam swept, rather than walked, out of the door, drawing Jan and Joanie in her wake. Outside, Beth saw them through the window huddling momentarily. Pam was still talking, only now she was preaching to the choir. Pam gesticulated, palms raised upwards. The others nodded their assent vigorously.

Chloe smiled, said something about being in touch soon, and headed outside.

Ying leaned over to Beth, who was still seated and feeling a bit stunned by the entire proceedings.

"I think you right", she indicated in her heavily accented English. "American schools much too easy for Chinese kids."

CHAPTER 6

"Our students are no longer Virginians competing against Iowans. They are competing against young people all over the world."
Mark Warner, Governor of Virginia

OCTOBER 2008

BRIGHTON, ENGLAND

Shannon Eyre kicked off her shoes and lay back on her bed. She was exhausted.

She was a sixth former, or the UK equivalent of a High School senior, at Padgett School in the suburbs of the seaside town of Brighton, south of London.

Like her peers in most of the rest of the industrialized world she was a few weeks into the most important and academically intensive year of her life. Already, she was realizing that the next few months were not going to be a barrel of laughs. In the following July she would sit her A-Level examinations. Other students her age in France would be burdened with study for the Baccalaureate, in Germany for the Abitur, in Australia for Board Exams.

In fact, in almost every one of the countries that were industrial competitors of the United States, independently graded examination boards were in place to make an accurate, objective, determination of what each student really knew before leaving school.

Shannon would be attempting Mathematics, Physics and Chemistry. Examinations in the two sciences would each involve a three hour written paper, a three hour laboratory practical, and a two hour multiple choice on separate days. A-levels were heavy duty examinations. A lot of the educational content that she would have to cover would be considered college level work in the United States. Furthermore, when exam time came, she would be required to be in command of all of the material that she had studied in the previous two years. No "cheat sheets" covered with useful formulas would be provided to make up for any gaps in her knowledge.

Her A-Level papers would not be graded by a sympathetic teacher with whom she had formed a relationship, and who might find it very difficult to render an unfavorable outcome.

Instead, they would be parceled up and sent off to a grading center where an anonymous "examiner" would apply completely intransigent standards and thereby determine, to a very large extent, Shannon Eyre's future.

Shannon knew, like all her peers, that her admission to college was predicated one hundred percent on her performance in these examinations. It was very simple. Don't do well enough on the A-levels, and you don't go to college. No system of appeal, no excuses that you didn't feel well that day, no matter that your references attested to the fact that you had single-handedly saved the planet from global warming, if you couldn't perform the calculus on your Mathematics paper then, next September, the college year would start without you. Too bad. Try again next year.

Not that there was anything sneaky or secretive about the process. Each student had been issued a book for each subject, at the beginning of the term, that showed the A-level examination papers from the last ten years. Shannon knew exactly the sort of thing that was coming at her next July. She also understood the depth of comprehension required of her, which rendered any charge that the exams involved 'teaching to the test' completely fatuous as far as A-levels were concerned.

Therein lay the reason for her exhaustion. For Shannon Eyre had made a careful study of the questions on the past papers in the book, and concluded that, eight months out, she knew very few of the answers.

Already, she was beginning to develop a distinct dislike for the bogeyman "independent examiner" that her teachers talked about so often. She had discovered that, when a test was given back, and one of her answers was marked wrong, there wasn't any point in arguing with the teacher that it was close enough to deserve credit.

"Shannon," Mrs. Larkins, the math teacher, would say. "Because I am familiar with how you work, I may know what you mean by what you wrote here, but the independent examiner won't have a clue. It's him that you have to convince of your knowledge, not me. And if you keep drawing your graphs in this haphazard fashion, you won't achieve that objective."

Shannon didn't like it, but she understood. Mrs. Larkins wasn't being mean by not giving her high grades. In fact the grades that Mrs. Larkins gave out didn't have any bearing on whether or not she obtained admission to a good university. The only thing that counted was what the "independent examiner" thought of her work. Mrs. Larkins was telling Shannon the truth, so that she knew what it would take to achieve eventual success. Grudgingly, Shannon had to admit that Mrs. Larkins was on her side. It was just "tough love".

Her options were straightforward, either hit the books or face a bleak future. She had opted for the former and embarked on a systematic campaign of study in the local public library. After school four nights each week she would spend two and a half hours there. There were no iPods, no Facebook, no cell phones ringing. Just solid study of all the properties of the elements in the periodic table, of Newton's Laws of Motion and how they impacted projectiles in flight, of Taylor and Maclaurin series expansions of trigonometric functions.

She was worn out – but slowly but surely she recognized that the sample examination papers in the book were beginning to make more sense to her.

SUNBURY, NEW HAMPSHIRE

On another bed, three thousand miles away, one of Shannon Eyre's age group peers also felt in need of some rest and relaxation.

In his case, though, there was no meaningful obstacle standing between him and a college placement.

"Oh, man," thought Bailey Hutchinson. "I have the worst case of senioritis. I simply cannot wait until next spring."

Bailey was already planning some serious "down" time for his final year of school. The trip to Cancun in February would undoubtedly be a highlight. Then there was senior skip day, the prom, and all those award nights when he and his classmates would have honors and scholarships showered on them by parents and teachers who were as anxious as Bailey to let the world see what a wonderful education the students had all received.

He planned to spend a lot of time after Christmas trying to perfect the jump shot which he hoped might land him on a college basketball team somewhere as a walk-on. High school ball would take a lot of time. Practice would last from three o'clock until five-thirty every day, and on away match days there would be many occasions when he wouldn't get home until after eight in the evening.

To accommodate his basketball, he had made sure that his course load would not be overwhelming. He had to take an English class to fulfill his requirements and had settled on a creative writing course. And he also needed a foreign language credit, and was taking an introductory Chinese class with a bunch of freshmen.

"I really don't get the big deal about foreign language," he told his friends. "I thought everyone in America was supposed to, like, speak English. Isn't it, like, our national language or something?"

Rounding out his schedule were electives in glass-cutting, photography and choir. He was done each day by twelve-thirty and took advantage of the senior early release privilege to head home for the afternoon.

His plan was simple. For the Fall semester he would use the time to research and prepare his college applications. Then in the Winter there would be basketball, and then it would be time for senior spring.

"Definitely best not to load up on too much academics with that lot going on," he thought to himself.

BRIGHTON, ENGLAND

It was not only Shannon Eyre who was feeling the pressure of A-levels. Jo Larkins, the math teacher knew that her reputation, also, depended on the results that her students achieved.

In the United States the high stakes nature of the examinations that Jo's students were about to sit would have sent every self respecting member of the educational establishment into an immediate coronary thrombosis. While the official line was that the stresses involved were counter productive to student learning, Jo, who had lived and worked briefly in America, knew that the real issue was that the US faculties vehemently opposed any sort of objective judgment being passed on their effectiveness as teachers.

She thought that was a shame. Having observed the systems on both sides of the Atlantic she had come down firmly on the side of the independent examiner model.

It was not that such a system didn't exist in America. It did. Jo had, in fact, taught there on an exchange program that was supposed to promote student participation in Advanced Placement or AP Examinations.

The AP Exams were equivalent, in many ways, to the A-levels for which she had prepared so many students over the years. That was actually the reason she had been selected for the exchange program. Like an A-level, the AP exam at the end of the year was graded by an independent examiner, not the student's teacher. The material that was in the curriculum was of a similar degree of difficulty to A-level, although Jo was interested to note, the AP problems tended to have a slightly more practical application. She thought, all in all, that the AP Calculus exam was based on an outstanding syllabus, and that any student who could answer the problems there satisfactorily would have an excellent basis of understanding to proceed to any sort of technical undergraduate course.

Students who took AP classes, at the school where she had worked in America, qualified for a bonus, or weighting, of their grade. So a "B" achieved in calculus was worth just as much to them on their grade point average as an "A" on an easier course. Jo suspected that some of her students were only in the class to obtain the weighting. She was particularly surprised to find out that many of the students had no intention whatsoever of sitting the AP exam at the end of the school year.

"What for?" asked one. "College admission is done by then. I got the class on my transcript, so the colleges will think I challenge myself. Besides, the exam's a lot of work and it wouldn't look good if I failed."

That was where the AP differed from the exams that students all over the rest of the world sat. The AP was certainly a demonstration of scholarship if you could pass it. It was graded on a scale of one to five, and most of the colleges gave you credit if you managed a four or five. But it wasn't required, and there was no real down side to not passing it. Only about fifteen percent of students even attempted an AP examination.

Jo thought the entire education system would work much better if AP were moved front and center in the process. But in America, the grade point average was still king.

She remembered the first time she had given a calculus test in a US high school. Some of the students had got most of it right and she had awarded them "A"s and "B"'s, some had got some of it right and had got "C"'s. Quite a few had got the whole lot wrong, had clearly paid no attention in class and hadn't handed in any homework and, to them, so she had doled out several "D"'s and "F"'s.

It had seemed like a reasonable strategy at the time. But the next day, the roof fell in. The kids who had got the bad grades sent in their secret weapons. Their Dads.

Three times that day Jo had been summoned to the principal's office. On each occasion, the body language of the parent sitting across the desk from the principal had told Jo what was coming before a word was spoken.

Pleasantries were not in evidence. Each parent got straight to the point.

"What kind of a teacher are you?" bellowed the first. "My kid wants to go to Harvard and that's hardly going to be possible if you're putting "F"'s on his damn transcript, is it?"

It didn't seem to matter that Jo had explained that out of the ten questions on the test, the student hadn't even attempted six, and had completely misunderstood the mathematical principles involved in the other four.

"It might have helped if he had handed in his homework over the past couple of weeks, so that I could have seen how he was absorbing the material," Jo explained, showing her grade book with the row of blank boxes indicating no work had been received from homework assignments.

"Now just hold on a minute," said Dad, getting progressively more irate. "Don't try to put all the blame on him. He's never had anything less than an "A" in any math class the whole time he's been in High School. It seems like the thing that is different here is you, not him."

That was a bit of a stunner to Jo. The student in question had shown a total lack of both ability and interest in her class. His test performance had consequently not come as a surprise to her. A couple of times when she had called on him in to answer questions in class, even though he hadn't raised his hand, he had seemed to struggle with basic algebraic techniques. It was far from clear to Jo that he should have even been in her calculus class. She couldn't imagine how he could possibly have demonstrated the capabilities to earn an "A" in pre-calculus the previous year.

It was the not the parent's anger, though, that had shaken Jo the most. Throughout the meeting the principal had sat with his fingers steepled on his chin, never once coming to her rescue. She felt very much as if she were being hung out to dry in a two against one situation.

"Fix this," the father had eventually threatened the principal, and stormed out without even looking at Jo. She had felt about two inches tall.

The message was repeated by each parent in more or less the same fashion over the course of the rest of the day.

The principal had closed the door after the third parent had left.

"Jo," he said, with what she considered a particularly condescending voice, one that was very different from the effusive welcome she had received from him when she had first reported for work a few weeks earlier. "I know you're new here, and indeed new to the education system in this country, but you don't seem to have got off to a very good start."

"The students in your calculus class are our best and brightest," he went on. "They are not used to receiving anything but the highest grades, and their parents, as you have seen, have sky high ambitions for them."

"Here in the United States the High School transcript is probably the single most important piece of information included in college applications. We need to be very sure that we are not doing our students a serious disservice by awarding lower grades than they might receive at other schools. That would put them at a major competitive disadvantage in the college admissions process."

Jo could hardly believe what she was hearing.

"So, are you telling me," she blurted out, incredulous. "That I should deliver grades that bear no relationship to the quality of the work performed?"

The principal had looked pained by that.

"Obviously not," he said. "But I would caution you against handing out much below a "B" in that class."

It was the end of the day. She had walked back to her empty classroom and sat, almost in tears.

"Obviously not...obviously not!" she thought. "You bastard. You just told me that I have to either compromise my academic integrity or get fired for alleged incompetence."

What frustrated her as much as anything was that she knew there was some logic in what she had been told. If the kids at the High Schools in the neighboring towns were being given "A"'s for lousy work, and she gave her students "D"'s and "F"'s for the same performance, then she probably was short changing them. The whole college admissions process, it seemed to her, boiled down to which teacher was willing to tell the biggest lies about their students' performance.

Reluctantly, she had "gone along to get along". Feeling like a complete fraud, she had graded on a scale that started at "A+" and ended at "B" for the rest of the year. Her popularity, and perceived skill as a teacher, soared, it seemed to her, in direct proportion to the average grade she handed out. There were no more visits from parents. The principal, too, treated her with a collegiality that was in marked contrast to the arms length approach he had employed when parents were complaining.

But, inside, she realized that she had become a full fledged member of a club to which she did not want to belong.

The students, of course, absent the motivating influence of the possibility of a poor grade, rarely exhibited the effort required to come to terms with the complex material she was teaching.

By the end of the school year she had had enough of kids who were far more interested in what letter she put on their transcript than they were in learning how to solve differential equations. Although her program was supposed to last for a second year, she had made some excuse about "personal and family reasons", and returned to Britain. At the staff meeting at the end of the year, the principal had said how sorry they all were to see her go. The superficiality of it all had made her want to throw up.

Back in Brighton, whenever a parent requested a meeting she thought back to her days in America. It was very different. In America she had been the gatekeeper, an adversary who could be bullied into writing a letter on a transcript that would allow a student to pass on to the next stage. In Europe, the parents knew that there was no point in bullying a teacher. She was an ally. The adversary was the independent examiner. And he couldn't be reached. So the meetings were all friendly, and the parents were supportive not threatening. If Jo handed out a low grade, the parents all knew that it only represented a valuable piece of advice, that things had to improve or the outcome on exam day was not going to be favorable. In Brighton, a poor test grade usually resulted in the student, not the teacher, getting kicked by the parent.

It could be nerve wracking when the A-level results were due. But it was a better model, she was convinced, not only for students but for teachers too.

SUNBURY, NEW HAMPSHIRE

Bailey Hutchins stirred from his afternoon nap.

His college applications were going quite well. He had already secured recommendations from his favorite teachers, who had all explained that while his raw intellect would put Albert Einstein to shame, his real achievement in life would likely be service to his fellow man that would make Nelson Mandela look like a war criminal.

Bailey was impressed by his own credentials. He hadn't realized what an impact he had made without really trying.

Despite Bailey's participation and high grade in the creative writing class, for the college essay his Dad had hired a writer from a website in India.

"Better not to leave anything to chance," he explained. "College admission is an important event in your life."

It was an amazing deal. For fifty bucks the Indian would write, it seemed to Bailey, an almost unlimited number of revisions. In fact, Bailey had even changed the title and theme of the piece on him a couple of times and asked that he start again. The next morning, there it was: a fresh crisp college application essay. Good stuff too.

The colleges would have to take notice. Especially when they saw all those "A"'s on his transcript.

CHAPTER 7.
"There is nothing either good or bad, but thinking make it so"
William Shakespeare, Playwright

OCTOBER 2008

SUNBURY ELEMENTARY SCHOOL, SUNBURY, NEW HAMPSHIRE

In principal Duncan Markwell's view of the world, new parents' evening was supposed to be a rather jolly affair. A time for everyone to agree on what a wonderful job he was doing.

The kids had been in school for several weeks now, and since, so far, none of his young charges had brained themselves by falling off the monkey bars in the playground, it seemed that there was every likelihood that this year's iteration of the event would be every bit as much of a love fest as previous celebrations. Duncan Markwell could take plenty of that.

As usual, he had ensured that both the superintendent and a school board member would be in attendance to hear the admiration, unleashed from both his own staff and the parents of his students, cascade down upon his head.

From the local school board, he had requested that long time board member Alice Farmington honor him with her presence.

Alice was in her sixth year on the board having handily won re-election for a second term a couple of years earlier. She would tell anyone who would listen about the huge time commitment associated with board membership, and how the small annual stipend represented a lot less than minimum wage when divided by the massive number of hours she logged on behalf of the community. Nevertheless, in reality, Alice would have given up her first born to human sacrifice rather than surrender her seat on the board.

There had been no other marked successes in Alice's personal or professional life. A large woman, no amount of time and make-up could transform her rather mean face into something worth looking at. And no huge promotions, no publications, or other triumphs had really singled her out for the sort of attention and respect that she craved above all else.

Her marriage had endured, mainly because of the children. But she had admitted to herself that there wasn't much spark left. That had left Alice to focus only on the kids' upbringing and her work on the board. So, every couple of weeks, when the gavel went down at the start of the board meetings, and the local TV cameras beamed her image to the community, that was Alice's moment. There was no way she was giving it up.

Since it was her firm intention to run again for another three year term, exposure at new parents meetings was definitely a political plus.

Alice was well aware that nearly all new parents arrived in the school system full of hope and goodwill. They all desperately wanted to believe that their child was going to receive "a good education" even if they all had different ideas as to what that meant, and how much effort and involvement it would require on their part.

They had experienced none of the bad test scores, peer bullying, or cutting from teams that occasionally embittered more long standing members of the community. Parent volunteerism was highest in the early grades, and declined steadily as students progressed through the system, mothers went back to work, and ennui set in.

For the new parents, the carefully constructed image of caring and success, developed through a public relations barrage lasting many years was, in nearly every case, their only exposure to the school district.

And Alice was determined that she would be the public face of that image.

In Sunbury, between the three elementary schools, almost four hundred children entered first grade each year. That meant eight hundred parents. Turnout for local elections was usually low. It only took about two thousand votes to retain a board seat. Her mentor, the board chairman Jim Mortensen, could be relied upon consistently to deliver several hundred from his political machine. Quite a few hundred more just came randomly because voters had no idea who any of the candidates were. So if she could pick up even half of the new parents it put her well on the way towards re-election.

So she sat on the stage in the gym where the meeting was being held, waiting for Markwell to open proceedings. Alternately she would try to look serious and involved, when approached by a teacher with some trivial question, and warm, as she beamed at parents arriving nervously in an unfamiliar setting.

Markwell allowed the clock to run about ten minutes past the allotted time for starting as the late-comers straggled in and took a seat at the back so as not to draw attention to their tardiness. Even so, only about half the chairs that his faithful cadre of volunteers from the PTA, supervised by the indomitable Pam Jackson, had laid out in neat rows were occupied when the principal patted the microphone and the hall hushed. Markwell was long used to low attendance at meetings and barely noticed any more. But to some of the parents, at their first school event, the patchwork of people amongst the empty chairs created an impression that maybe not many folks cared about what happened. Which was true.

"Welcome, welcome, welcome!" Duncan Markwell beamed at his audience. No-one was going to escape tonight without knowing that he was a nice guy.

That was actually the case. If you scraped your knee in school, and had to go to the nurse's office, the principal was genuinely concerned, and not just because the injury might generate a complaint. He really did want to ensure the well being of those in his care. He just didn't think that the rate at which they learned Mathematics, or the quality of their essays, mattered as much as the epidermis over their kneecaps. The guy would have been a perfect candidate for manager of a day-care center.

"First let me say how absolutely thrilled we are to have the privilege of you entrusting your children to us here at Sunbury Elementary."

Sitting in the crowd, next to her husband who had been reluctantly dragged along, Beth Southwick thought to herself, "I didn't know we had a choice!"

Next came the obligatory self-deprecating jokes. After briefly introducing himself, and making sure everyone knew he was the head honcho, Markwell made some crack as to how, because of his wonderful team in attendance that evening, there wasn't much more for him to do but sit and listen while they did all the work. A polite titter of laughter rippled around the hall. On the stage the group of teachers laughed too, on average, slightly louder than the parents. Several of them, though, despite their grins were thinking that Markwell had just described what happened pretty much every day at Sunbury Elementary. Amongst his staff, Markwell's ability to vanish into his office with his Dunkin Donuts coffee was legendary.

Before the teachers got the chance to take over with the rest of the agenda, however, some serious ass-kissing was in order. Markwell was certain not to miss the opportunity of having a board member and the superintendent captive on the same stage in his gymnasium.

"But first, let me introduce you to some important folks in the school district who I'm honored to have with us tonight."

Markwell loved microphones. He sometimes wondered whether he should have been in the theatre. He could surely put on a show.

"To my left," he continued. "Is school board member Alice Farmington. A board member for five years, and twice voted board member of the year. It is to Alice that we are particularly indebted for the initiative that has led to the lowering of class size across the district during that period."

Alice raised her hand and waved her agenda at the crowd. She did her best to contort her face into what passed as a smile for her, and was rewarded with a smattering of applause that died away far too quickly for her liking. Clearly nobody in the audience had ever heard of her.

Douglas leaned over to Beth.

"So she's the reason the tax rate has been going up so much," he whispered. Douglas had a way of getting to the bottom of things financially. If the class size was going down, then the number of teachers, and the cost, must be going up. If it wasn't producing any improvement in test scores, then it was far from clear to Douglas why this board member should be winning awards and acclaim, or why anyone should think smaller class sizes were a great idea.

"Ssshh," hissed Beth, smiling. But actually she wished someone would say the same thing out loud.

"And while we're on that subject." Markwell paused.

"What do I got here?"

Beth winced. Douglas breathed in sharply. Whether they liked it or not, the individual responsible for the formative years of their children's education was someone who saw nothing untoward in butchering the English language in front of an audience.

Looking up, Beth noticed a momentary frown cross Alice Farmington's face.

"She caught it, too," Beth thought. "But wasn't going to show anything."

Neither the superintendent, nor any of the teachers, missed a beat.

From behind his seat, Markwell pulled a large sheet of cardboard, turned it with a flourish and stood it on an easel that was set up in front of him and to his right. It partly blocked the view of the superintendent who ostentatiously shifted his chair to get a better view. Everyone chuckled. Markwell grimaced as though he had just committed a major faux pas.

The forced jocularity of it all was getting on Beth's nerves a bit.

"This is the artist's rendition of the new elementary school that the community will vote on next Spring." announced Markwell, with a hushed reverence that suggested that the picture held almost religious significance for him.

"And now I'd like to introduce Dr. Miles Hamlin, our marvelous district superintendent, who was also honored as New Hampshire Superintendent of the Year in 2006. Dr. Hamlin will just take a minute to explain the significance of this building, and what a milestone it will be in the educational futures of your children if the voters approve the investment next year."

Markwell sat. Another smattering of applause broke out. It was apparent that some of the audience would rather hear about what was happening to their kids than about yet one more thing that would probably raise their taxes.

The superintendent got to his feet, almost knocking over the easel in front of him. That brought a more genuine sounding peel of laughter.

Dr. Miles Hamlin was, like all school district superintendents, a grandmaster of the playing of the game.

At fifty-two years old, his ascent to his current position, which he had held for four years, had followed a fairly typical path. After college, and a Masters in special education, there had been some teaching experience, which in his case was social studies to middle school students.

Then he had embarked on his Ph.D. His thesis had been a landmark paper aimed at showing the benefits of mixed ability classrooms. After two years of extensive study, he was dismayed to find that the data that he had so assiduously accumulated did not support his hypothesis. Rather than adjust his conclusions, he had manipulated the data and published his results to great acclaim from the educational establishment. Nobody ever went back to check on the validity of the numbers, and the study had propelled his career to its present heights.

There was no salary scale for superintendents, and he negotiated his contract directly with the board and their attorneys. So having a board that looked favorably upon his efforts enabled him to add all manner of sweeteners whenever it was time to renegotiate. In particular, like many senior local officials, he had several golden parachute clauses that would ensure that his final year of employment, whether it ended with resignation or dismissal, was spectacularly lucrative. Since pensions were based on final year's income, that would, one day, substantially enhance the amount of annual retirement income that he would be entitled to for the rest of his life.

Right now, the thing that would make the board see him in the best light was if he could help to persuade the community to add another building to its already somewhat bloated inventory of physical plant. Board members just loved new buildings. It meant groundbreaking ceremonies with photos in the newspaper and visits from the governor. Perhaps even more important, it enabled them to claim that they were far too busy with choosing the color of the carpets to pay attention to how many of their students could not answer simple math problems correctly.

"We've got a building to open, you know," they would respond with barely checked incredulity that anyone might seek to focus on anything else at such an important time.

So Hamlin stood front and center on the stage before the new parents, ready to give it the old college try one more time. On whose behalf he was really doing it, though, was less than certain.

"Thanks Duncan, for that kind introduction," he said. "And good evening Ladies and Gentlemen, thank you, too, for coming out tonight."

"And while we're on the subject of awards," he smiled. "We shouldn't forget that Principal Markwell was New Hampshire Elementary School Principal of the Year last year."

The applause was even more grudging.

"So many awards, so little learning," Douglas whispered under his breath.

"You are all here tonight," Hamlin went on. "Because, as you should, you want to learn as much as possible about the educational experience that your children will have with us for what we hope will turn out to be the next twelve years."

"As new parents this year, you are in the unique position of standing to gain the most from the investment that the district is proposing," he went on.

"There's that word again," thought Beth, "Investment. It's never 'spending' when it's something they will control."

Her mind went back to the article that Mortensen had written slamming school choice vouchers. She was pretty sure he had referred to those as "spending" not "investment".

Hamlin was droning on. Beth noticed several parents stifling yawns.

"The building is a significant component of the strategic master plan that we have been following now for a number of years. Since it will allow us to move our fifth grade out of the middle school and back into the elementaries, it will decrease class size in all of the first eight grades."

"Studies have shown that decreasing class size is a critical component in improving educational outcomes."

Beth knew by now that that one was a whopper. The island nation of Singapore regularly achieved some of the highest student achievement levels in the world. And their average class size was around fifty! In New Hampshire, over the last ten years, there had been a school building boom. The huge amounts of additional capacity added had not been in response to an increase in enrollment. That had been flat.

What had happened was that, as in several other states, the state Supreme Court had legislated from the bench in favor of increasing state and local spending on education. In New Hampshire that had resulted from interpreting the constitutional phrase, "cherish the interests of literature and the sciences" to mean that the state must increase its previously fairly small contribution to public schools by a factor of about eight. Students in private schools did not receive any cherishing.

The resulting windfall from the state to communities lowered local taxes slightly and was portrayed to voters by the school districts as free money, even though the state had taken the money out of the pockets of the same people who had been paying the local taxes in the first place. In actuality, the court decision was a financial wash for most taxpayers, until the districts started spending on their favorite toys. New buildings.

Since new classrooms were being added and there were no new students, obviously class size fell. Hamlin, and superintendents and board members all over the state claimed victory. Nobody ever bothered to look at the actual outcome.

When the classrooms were added, there was a corresponding need for more teachers. Since the number of good teachers was finite, that meant scraping the bottom of the barrel so that less effective teachers were hired to fill the extra job slots. So even though the class size went down, student access to the best teachers was diluted.

Having a good teacher at the front of the room is one thing that all sides of the education debate agree upon as being a driver of sound outcomes. Given that that was happening less frequently, it should have come as no surprise to anyone that, despite an approximate doubling in overall per student cost in the decade following the Supreme Court rulings, there had been no measurable improvement whatsoever in student performance.

Beth wondered what would have happened if the Supreme Court had ordered that all the extra money be spent on vouchers and private schools instead. It seemed that with perhaps the best of intentions, the justices had nevertheless backed completely the wrong horse.

The audience stirred a little from its somnolence. Hamlin was showing signs of tiring and hopefully might sit down soon. He had already explained that the proposed building was a marvel of modern engineering, containing all the necessary functionality, but somehow miraculously pared to the bone in terms of cost. Actually he concluded, the building committee had shown that it would really only add a few pennies to the tax rate.

Douglas snorted. "Rubbish."

Hamlin exhorted everyone to support the project, gave some contact information for anyone who would like to join in with the public relations effort to sell the initiative to the community, and sat down to another half-hearted round of applause. Alice Farmington, though, was nodding that she approved of his remarks. Hamlin felt good about that.

Markwell got his hands on the microphone again and explained the rest of the evening's agenda. Several teachers were going to present details of the instructional programs.

First up were the Math team. Beth found this slightly ironic since there had been practically no evidence of any Math lessons at all since the beginning of the school year.

Three Sunbury elementary teachers had been selected as the presenters. The one thing that characterized their presentation was color. Charts, lots of charts, were set up on the stage.

Douglas stirred and paid more attention than he had for the previous quarter of an hour. He had been a Math major in college. He wanted his kids to be competent in the subject.

The presentation took about ten minutes. It was clear that the philosophy of learning that Beth had observed on her visit to the classroom extended even to this most formal of subjects. The teachers described a learning environment that was full of gimmicks and toys. There were all sorts of little pieces of plastic, called manipulatives. There seemed to be a total absence, though, of anything like concrete Math facts.

The presenter was a second grade teacher named Paula Verdi. She was another graduate of the Central New Hampshire teacher training program.

"In this subject, we particularly want to encourage critical thinking skills, and data analysis." Verdi rambled on, "Rather than focusing on the old methods of rote learning we want our students to be discriminating readers of numerical information. So for instance, as they get older we will present them with information about social

44

issues like global warming and world poverty and ask them to draw inferences from data and graphs as to what it means to their lives."

Douglas snorted again. "Oh God, rain forest algebra!" He muttered under his breath so that only Beth could hear.

"If that's what you think, then why don't you say it out loud?" Beth whispered to him.

But Douglas just sat staring straight ahead. So did everyone else.

"Studies have shown that when we involve children in real world problem solving situations that they develop a much deeper understanding of the subject in the long term." The stream of glib one liners continued unabated.

"For instance," she held up a text book. "Whereas in the old days a problem might have asked children an addition problem, like three plus four, now it is enriched."

She read from the book. "If Juan has four balls, and Bonita has three, how many balls do they have altogether. Then we use finger counting to teach technique, rather than rote learning of three plus four."

This was too much for Beth. She thought back to her commitment to herself and her kids that she had made on the porch a few days ago. Barely realizing what she was doing, she put up her hand. The old fear of being the center of attention rose up in her throat. She knew her voice was going to sound strained.

Douglas glanced across at her slightly quizzically. He knew her well enough to recognize a mild panic in her body language. He sighed.

Duncan Markwell noticed Beth's arm go up and signaled his recognition to her. When Paula Verdi momentarily ran out of platitudes, Markwell stood and said, "Paula, I think we have a question."

Beth stood.

"Hi, I'm Beth Southwick. I have a child just starting in first grade. I've been a bit surprised, actually, at the lack of a formal daily math class."

To Beth her own voice sounded as if it was coming from someone else.

But a murmur of assent came from some members of the audience. Beth felt emboldened.

"Also," she went on. "He already knows, and I'm sure a lot of the other kids do too, that three and four make seven. And in fact that twenty-three and thirty-four make fifty seven. I don't think he needs Juan and Bonita, or even Jack and Jill for that matter, to explain it further. I was just wondering when we might be starting on something he doesn't yet know, like multiplication."

45

Beth dropped back into her seat. Her heart was racing. She didn't know if she had made a fool of herself, or sounded arrogant. Nevertheless, she couldn't deny a certain elation. On behalf of her children she had faced her deepest personal fears and spoken up in public. When she had felt just a glimmer of support from the audience, it had imbued her instantly with a sense of authority that she had never previously experienced.

Later she would recognize that it was called leadership.

There was a momentary silence in the room. Douglas looked around. It was a bit like one of those war movies when someone pulls the pin on a grenade and then drops it, so that nobody knows which unfortunate character it will end up next to when it explodes.

He noticed an enormous variety of reactions to this seemingly fairly innocuous question.

On the stage Alice Farmington's facial features narrowed even more than usual, if that was possible. Markwell looked annoyed that his command performance had been marred by a first question that failed to reflect the love and affection for his school that he worked so hard to cultivate. Superintendent Hamlin just looked bored, questions like this one just unnecessarily extended the proceedings.

Paula Verdi was clearly in a blind panic. This wasn't in the script. They hadn't told her at Central NH that some folks might not agree with her "best practices".

Pam Jackson, taking her cue from "Duncan" and "Alice", looked ready to explode. She knew this girl was trouble from the start.

A reporter from the local paper was scribbling notes in his pad, presumably thinking that it might turn out, after all, to have been worth the effort of responding to Markwell's request for press coverage of the event. Nothing like a little discord in town to attract readership. Markwell noticed his scribbling and was even more irritated, he made a mental note to let the newspaper editor know not to send that particular reporter again.

Quite a few of the audience though, particularly the fathers in attendance, seemed to welcome the question.

Since Paula Verdi still had her mouth open but didn't appear to be about to say anything, her colleague on the presentation team, Suzanne Hayes, stepped in to help her out.

"Well, that's a very good question," her voice was soothing, the tension was reduced a notch or two immediately. "Thank you for asking it."

"First of all I want to assure you that there is in fact a great deal of Mathematics instruction going on in school everyday."

"Good old Suzanne," thought Markwell. "Experience counts."

"At this phase of the school year, the most important thing for our professional staff is to conduct a thorough evaluation of each student's readiness for first grade. So although you may not have seen something that you might think of as a traditional Mathematics lesson, in fact valuable learning is occurring all of the time, and the teachers are observing very carefully, during 'exploring time', just how your child relates to mathematical concepts. For example, by how he uses the manipulatives that Paula was describing."

"Bullshit," muttered Douglas. "Probably scratches his nose with them."

"As to the second part of your question, relating to multiplication," Hayes carried on. "Many studies have shown that the cognitive capabilities of first graders are not sufficiently developed for that concept. We can actually do a lot more harm than good by trying to push the pace beyond what the students are really ready for. At this point we are just trying to make sure that a basic foundation of numerical understanding is present that we can build on so that they become lifelong learners. That's all part of the 'Learning Through Discovery' philosophy. Does that answer your question?" Suzanne Hayes concluded with a winning smile.

Beth thought, "Not really." But nodded anyway. It was a good job that they were going to be "lifelong learners" anyway. At the pace they were going that's how long it would take to get to anything useful.

Sitting on the other side of the hall, Chloe Roberts had enjoyed the exchange enormously, and the obvious discomfort that it had caused the administrators on the stage. When she had met Beth at the Bagel shop she had clearly detected the undercurrent of dissatisfaction that Beth had with what was going on in the classroom. But she had not been sure whether Beth had the motivation to carry it further than a mother's union meeting.

"Apparently she does," Chloe thought to herself. "Interesting."

The Math presentation thus concluded rather awkwardly, and a separate set of teachers rose to explain the English program. Although the subject had changed the theme appeared the same. There were multiple technical sounding terms that were employed mainly, it seemed to Beth, to create an excuse for not insisting that all children should become effective readers as soon as possible.

The benefits of "whole language" and a "literature rich" environment were extolled to the detriment of the "old fashioned phonics method". Beth thought she had read somewhere that literacy rates were higher in the eighteenth century than in modern day America. It seemed that maybe "old fashioned phonics" worked fairly well back then. And why was "literature rich" such a brilliant new idea anyway. What else could you read?

But she didn't raise her hand again.

The presenters looked at each other to confirm that they had all said their piece, and turned to sit down without inviting questions.

Chloe Roberts raised her hand. She had heard the catch in Beth's voice, and knew that it had taken an act of will from her to ask her question. If she was willing to face her demons like that, she deserved some support. Chloe had been around local politics a little more than Beth, knew all the players, and didn't feel the same anxiety about public speaking. In fact, she had a certain disdain for the motives of the town's educational leaders that made it easy for her to get on her feet and speak in front of a crowd.

"Are we taking more questions?" Markwell asked the teachers, looking at his watch. He was a bit gun-shy after what had happened a few minutes earlier, "Time is getting on a bit."

"Yes, I'd be happy to," replied one of the presenters, whose name was Sarah Mercer.

"Idiot," thought Markwell. "Haven't I taught you anything."

"Hi, I'm Chloe Roberts. I was just wondering," began Chloe. "What the benefit of showing quite so many movies might be?"

Sarah Mercer, just like Paula Verdi before her, got the deer in the headlights look.

"Well," she said. "Sometimes there are important themes in movies."

Chloe was still on her feet.

"Yes, granted," she continued. "But after we've got the theme from Land Before Time, do the children also need to spend classroom time watching Land Before Time 2, and Land Before Time 3. Are the themes very different. What is the theme in Land Before Time anyway?"

The reporter was making notes again. Enough was enough. Markwell jumped to the microphone.

"I think that's one you should take up with the classroom teacher," he wore his warmest smile, but inside he was seething. This was not how new parents night was supposed to turn out at all.

"Folks, it's getting late, I want to thank everyone again for coming, and I can't tell you how much we're looking forward to working with you and your children over the next few years. Have a safe journey home. Goodnight."

The parents got up and headed for the exits.

The next morning, despite the glorious weather there was a dark cloud on Markwell's psychological horizon. One that appeared every few years and threatened the battlements of his carefully constructed citadel.

He had felt cornered the previous night by the questioners who had voiced concerns about lack of academic challenge in the classrooms that he supervised. He had particularly sensitive antennae for that sort of thing and he was fairly sure the two mothers were in cahoots. He had been relieved to note, though, that they had sat apart and did not appear to be a part of a large organized group. Experience told him that there was reason to hope that their complaint would be slow to coalesce politically, and that embarrassment over airing opinions in public would prevent any escalation.

In the privacy of his office, where he controlled the levers of power, he pulled his file of first grade class lists and located the names of the children whose parents had asked the questions.

It was no surprise to him to discover that they were in the same class. He had guessed that the mothers probably hatched the plot at a wretched class parent meeting at the coffee shop. In a candid moment, even he would have had to admit that Jenny Jones really didn't hack it in the classroom. He was certainly glad that there weren't any teachers like her at his children's school. But you couldn't get rid of staff just because of that. The slightest hint of a suggestion of incompetence in a teacher's performance could create enormous problems for him with the union.

He took a blank sheet of paper and wrote down the names of the relevant students and attached it to Jenny's class page in his file. He didn't need to commit any explanation to paper. Next summer, when he was preparing class groupings for the following year, he would come across the paper and would remember its provenance. His mind worked that way. Those two students would never find themselves together in the same classroom in his school again. The mothers would be making new friends at the coffee shop next year.

CHAPTER 8
"Human kind cannot bear too much reality."
T. S. Eliot, Poet and Playwright

OCTOBER 2008

RUSSELL SENATE BUILDING, WASHINGTON DC

Miller time. Remains of the day. Whatever it was, the evening hour wasn't bringing any of the expected entitlement of relief to Senator John St. Cloud, Republican of New Hampshire. Although, as a senator, he had long ago mastered the art of presenting an impenetrable façade of confidence to the outside world, the truth was that the job just churned his gut. It churned from the moment he awoke in the morning until sleep or a large shot of whisky stilled his senses at night. His Dad had been more of a natural, unfazed by reality.

He leaned back in his patent leather chair. The office was quiet. The staff had gone to the softball game on the Mall. He'd stroll down there later on to see how they were doing.

He pushed his glasses up on his forehead, and massaged his face. It didn't help.

"This is just never going to work," he admitted to himself for the umpteenth time. As he had been doing everyday for the last year or two.

When the financial crash that New Hampshire's Senator St. Cloud had been privately predicting for years finally arrived it was not the slow steady decline that he had expected.

After Lehman Brothers declared bankruptcy out of the blue on September 15th, the graph of the Dow Jones Index looked like the arc of those Chinese high board divers he had watched in the Beijing Olympics during the summer. It hung as if suspended momentarily, then in the first week of October went down in a parabolic arc of ever increasing steepness.

The self proclaimed 'Masters of the Universe' on Wall Street were exposed as nothing more than a bunch of bookies who hadn't been smart enough to cover their bets. Then again, maybe they were smart after all. When the dice turned up the wrong numbers for them, they simply gave the task of paying off their losses to the American taxpayer.

Insurance companies, most notably AIG, had bet trillions of dollars on the ability of American home owners to repay their mortgages. But too many of the mortgages had been provided on an adjustable rate basis. Compounding the problem was that, thanks to Congress' hopeful sounding Community Reinvestment Act, banks had been pressured to lower their lending standards to higher risk borrowers. When the interest rates on the mortgages reset upwards, and the payments increased dramatically, the number of defaults went off the charts. It wouldn't have been so bad if the only people betting were the folks holding the lousy paper. But the odds being offered by the insurance companies looked so good to all sorts of other speculators that they wanted a piece of the action too. While the mortgages were still being paid, the insurance companies were happy to take the bets, and let the good times roll. Bonuses all round for the boys, mansions in the Hamptons, first class flights, fancy restaurants. Life was good.

But when the monumental pile of unsustainable debt all came tumbling down, there wasn't nearly enough left in the insurance company kitties to pay out all the winners who had bet on precisely that outcome.

The normal bankruptcy laws were deemed completely inadequate to handle the crash of gigantic financial empires. The only institution on the horizon that was remotely financially sufficient to plug up the gaps was the United States Government. So the government was preparing to whip out the limitless credit card, otherwise known as the national debt, and borrow a few trillion more from the Chinese.

It was ironic really. The solution chosen to repair a mess caused by a mountain of unsustainable debt was to create another mountain of unsustainable debt. St. Cloud knew it was all smoke and mirrors. The financial gurus might succeed in temporarily putting Humpty Dumpty back together again. But it would all come crashing down again. All of America's conspicuous consumption was being done with borrowed money. Sooner or later there had to be a day of reckoning.

The root cause of the problem was that the country was living beyond its means. And that couldn't be fixed by some fiscal sleight of hand.

His Republican colleague John McCain of Arizona had previously accused the Congress of "spending like drunken sailors". He was wrong of course. Drunken sailors could only spend the money they had in their pockets. The United States was doing it all on the come. With a $10 trillion national debt, it had accumulated by far the biggest pile of IOU's in the history of the planet. It represented about thirty thousand dollars for every man, woman and child in America.

What was worse, St. Cloud knew that that figure was only the beginning. Annual federal deficits were adding to the problem at about a thousand dollars per person per year. Bad enough in and of itself, but the eight hundred pound gorilla was still hiding in the tall grass of future financial predictions.

The aging baby boomers were hitting retirement and tipping the ratios of contributors to beneficiaries to a place that FDR had never conceived of when the very first Social Security check for $22.54 was made out to Ida May Fuller on January 31st, 1940.

In 1940, there were about forty people paying into Social Security for every person receiving benefits. Fast forward to the present day and it had become about three to one. At some point in the next thirty or forty years, depending on whose actuary you believed, it would become two to one and the whole deck of cards would come tumbling down.

He smiled to himself. In a private moment his Dad had once revealed to him the holy grail of politics. It was a phrase the old man had heard while watching a news clip on TV about the art of "hog calling". The newly crowned world champion was describing how to get a herd of hogs to come running when he yelled at them. The secret, the champ revealed, was that, "You gotta convince them hogs you got something for them."

FDR and the Congress of the day must have known the secret too. Ida May Fuller had paid a total of $22 into the system during the interval between the inception of Social Security and her retirement. She got the whole lot back in the first check, eventually lived to be a hundred years old, and drew out a total of $22,000. FDR was elected president four times.

It was the world's biggest Ponzi scheme. New recruits got promises of future hand-outs, and in return they paid those already in the plan. Any corporate CEO trying something similar with a corporate pension plan would have the FBI knocking on his door with the handcuffs. It was just amazing how many of the public still thought there was a vault full of hundred dollar bills, with their own name on, already stashed safely away. The Social Security Trust Fund. It sounded solid and reliable. Too bad it didn't actually exist.

He chuckled as he remembered how just a few years earlier there had been projections of a gigantic federal surplus appearing early in the 21st century. Much hot air had been exuded planning on what should be done with the excess money. President Clinton pursing his lip and telling the nation to, "Save social security first".

What a joke! Even the most wildly optimistic estimates of the surplus only came to a few hundred billion dollars. Social security needed tens of trillions before it could be considered a fully funded pension plan. Estimates varied wildly, but he liked to use the fairly conservative one of a shortfall of sixty trillion dollars over the next fifty years. He chose that one because it was divisible conveniently by the three hundred million people in the United States. Only problem was that the division yielded two hundred thousand per head. So in other words, a young family of four starting out today with a mortgage and car loans was also on the hook for the best part of a million bucks in social security expenses over their lifetimes, over and above what they were already paying.

A triple whammy was about to hit. First the change in the ratio of contributors to beneficiaries, then the change in life expectancy of retirees. And finally, perhaps the biggest unknown of all, the skyrocketing costs of medical care. Put all of those together, stir thoroughly and what did you get? The potential for social anarchy on an unprecedented scale.

Either the benefits were going to have to be reduced to almost nothing, or the payroll taxes were going to have to be doubled, or tripled.

"How will that play in Peoria?" he wondered. "Probably depends on how many old folks, and how many young people there are in Illinois."

In America, guns comfortably outnumbered people. The prospect of millions of angry impoverished old folks, armed to the teeth and protesting the diminished benefits that they would see as the theft of their entitlement to their golden years, made him shudder.

The only remotely equally scary prospect was millions of young people, also armed to the teeth, protesting higher taxes and what they would see as the theft of their entitlement to a turn at the American dream.

"God knows, they think they're entitled to everything else."

He mentally plotted the graph of the timeline of his own planned trajectory towards the presidency, and the much more catastrophic financial meltdown which he was now certain was in America's future. If he was president when the crash came, neither a second term nor a favorable legacy were very likely, to say the least. Hell, in that instance, it would be like one of those event horizons that the physicists talked about. Impossible to predict what lay on the other side. A political forecaster's black hole.

Better try and do the whole presidential thing quickly. 2012 maybe, certainly no later than 2016. Then he'd be done by 2024. They could probably play the smoke and mirrors game until then. "Better keep them hogs in the dark if you don't have anything for them." But when it came to the crunch, whose side would he take? Young or old? It didn't seem as though skin color was going to matter much anymore. The great national political division of the 21st century was going to depend on one thing, and one thing only – age.

He glanced down at his desk. There was a memo on top of his "in" tray left by a staffer on her way out the door to the ball game. The Department of Education didn't have much better to do with their time than send out a proliferation of meaningless memos. This one related to the importance of all Congressmen understanding a recent report that showed how beneficial it was to have "Black Women's Studies" in high school curricula. Of course, it would need some additional federal funding to achieve that.

Over the years a few half hearted attempts had been made to get rid of the Department of Education. St. Cloud thought it would be a good thing. No government agency was remotely as politicized, and most of the department's efforts were directed towards the sole aim of supporting the monopoly position of its friends teaching in the public schools.

St. Cloud was under no illusions about the public schools in the United States. Not one single member of Congress currently had a child enrolled in the Washington, DC public system. That pretty much said it all right there.

He had for a long time considered that the most shameful act of the Clinton presidency had not occurred with Monica Lewinsky under the desk in the Oval Office. Rather it had happened the day that Clinton had stood with Al Gore in the Rose Garden, pursed his lips and jutted his chin one more time, and announced that he would veto the law that Congress had passed to allow a school choice voucher program in the capital.

The program would have allowed a small number of underprivileged kids in the District a chance to escape from the dangerous and under performing public schools, and to obtain their publicly funded education at a privately run institution of the parents' choosing.

There were over sixty private schools in the District of Columbia where annual fees were less than what it cost to add a child to the bloated public school system. By any sane and rational business argument it made sense to use them as providers of publicly financed education. But Clinton had sided with the monopolists of the public system.

While Clinton spoke, daughter Chelsea and a couple of the Gore kids were taking lessons at the very private Sidwell Friends School just down the road. If you were looking for political hypocrisy, try that one on for size.

School choice vouchers should have been the ultimate platform issue for the Democrats. Equal opportunity was stamped all over the concept. Vouchers would take away the built in advantage that wealthy kids possessed because their parents could afford private school fees.

It was, however, one of the supreme ironies of political life that as soon as a Republican got the first syllable of the word "voucher" out of his mouth he was instantly lambasted by every Democrat in earshot.

St. Cloud knew the reason well. The long reach of the teachers' unions. Their two million members were almost universally aligned with the Democratic Party. Not only that, but those members were amongst the most politically active group of people in the country.

Money talked. And when it came to money, his esteemed colleagues on the other side of the aisle were perfectly happy to throw their constituents' children on the mercy of truly appalling inner city public schools rather than risk offending political contributors in the union.

"What a world," he thought.

The unions feared one thing above all else. The loss of their monopoly. As long as they controlled all of the kids and all of the money, they also controlled the ideology that permeated the classroom. They could keep science out and global warming in. Self esteem, political correctness, the rain forest and ethno-centric curricula, could reign supreme over calculus and Shakespeare. In short, they could turn the nation's public schools into little factories churning out Democratic voters. Independent thought could be all but eliminated.

It was social engineering on a grand scale. Only the wealthy could escape by effectively buying their way out into private schools with higher academic standards.

Between federal, state and local funding, around $500 billion dollars was being spent annually on public education, an amount approximating to the defense budget. It was producing astonishingly little in the way of tangible results. Even in relatively prosperous states like his own, only a tiny percentage of public high school graduates could speak a foreign language or perform calculus reliably. In some of the blighted inner cities of the nation, hardly anyone made it all the way to 12th grade and those that did often struggled to read.

Colleges were offering courses in remedial reading and math to ever increasing numbers of students.

"For God's sake, how do you maintain your credibility as an institution of higher learning when you're conferring degrees on people who can't read properly," he rubbed his eyes again.

The unions had several gold standard non-negotiable policies. One of them was opposition to any form of independent testing of students. It was hardly surprising. If you hold a monopoly, the last thing you want is any objective measurement of how poorly you are serving your customers.

"Or prisoners depending on your point of view," chuckled St. Cloud out loud to himself.

A limited amount of testing, nevertheless, managed to survive the union's opposition. The most interesting results were the ones that compared the performance of students in the United States to students elsewhere in the world. Those tests generated league tables ranking performance by country. That seemed to St. Cloud like a fairly reliable predictor of national economic success in the future.

The United States invariably appeared close to the bottom of all international comparisons. The public school lobby equally invariably claimed that the tests were racially biased, insensitive, "just one test on one day", "geared towards rote learning" and subject to sample error in the selection of students tested. Having dismissed the results thus, and possessing no competitors in their field of providing publicly funded education, they went right back to the same classroom techniques that had produced the results in the first place.

It was certainly a gloomy picture.

"The politician's dilemma," he thought. He knew that the only solution rested on the use of vouchers and high stakes testing to create a marketplace that measured, recognized and valued high performance in schools. Yet for him to openly promote such a program was to bring down a political firestorm upon himself. Active opposition from the unions, and their friends in the media, would likely preclude his elevation to the one political office with sufficient power to push through such a huge change.

The conclusion was stark and obvious. If he wanted to be president, he had better keep his mouth shut about education.

A much better way to get elected was to make absurd, completely undeliverable promises about maintaining the standard of living of everyone in America by ever increasing government largesse. Never mind that, as Margaret Thatcher had once famously pointed out, "The problem with socialism is that eventually you run out of someone else's money."

He rose stiffly from his chair and prepared to head out to the softball game on the mall. He picked up the Wall Street Journal and was just about to dump it in the trash when he noticed one of the recent international comparison tests, like the ones that had just occupied his thoughts, printed on the front page.

This one had placed American students just ahead of their Jordanian peers, but miles behind anywhere that possessed indoor toilets, in arithmetical reasoning amongst fifteen year olds.

"Great," thought St. Cloud to himself. "If all else fails we can rest safe in the knowledge that we could build an economy around becoming the world's low cost producer of goats' cheese. With our relative advantage in intellect, we'll beat the living crap out of Jordan economically and fifty million geriatric Americans will live out their waning years in luxury off the profits."

In particular, if the schools kept on focusing on self-esteem instead of knowledge, skills and capabilities, then the party was over for America.

He tossed the paper in disgust and turned out the lights. Senator St. Cloud, aspirant to the Presidency, possessed a disarmingly simple education strategy. Punt.

CHAPTER 9
"If you tell a lie big enough and keep repeating it, people will eventually come to believe it."
Joseph Goebbels, Nazi Propaganda Minister

OCTOBER 2008

SUNBURY, NEW HAMPSHIRE

Beth was not used to confrontation and disliked it intensely. It took her several days to fully recover her emotional equilibrium after the antagonism that had occurred at the coffee shop. Doug had christened it the "The Battle of the Bagel" when she had told him what had happened.

But nevertheless the issue was now playing continuously in her mind and all sorts of questions that she hadn't really considered before kept bubbling to the forefront.

In particular, Pam's parting comment about sending children to private school.

Why was it that just because Pam obviously liked what was going on in the public system, they all had to agree? Why should it have to be the same for everyone, when clearly they all thought differently? Pam thought test scores didn't matter, Beth thought that getting the right answer was more important than self esteem and exploring time. How could their children possibly get an education, of which both she and Pam approved, in the same classroom? Or even in the same school?

And why was it that just because education was a public expense it meant that everyone had to go to the school where all the teachers were public employees? The more she thought about this last one the angrier she started to get. Government bought all sorts of things from private companies. Why not education too? If it was a lot cheaper to send a child to Chertsey than to keep adding them into the public school then why not use Chertsey as a private provider of a publicly funded education?

She was becoming more and more certain that the op-ed writer, who had been so lambasted in the paper for venturing forth with what sounded like an entirely reasonable idea, was in fact correct. She made up her mind she would find out more about these "vouchers".

It was while she was turning the thought over and over in her mind one afternoon that the phone rang. It was Chloe Roberts, who Beth had considered luke warm in her support at the "Battle of the Bagel", but who had asked the "Land Before Time" question at the parents' meeting.

"I've been thinking about what you said the other morning, and, frankly, I agree with you. I've been feeling a bit bad that I didn't stand up for you a bit more. That Pam's pretty fierce though isn't she?"

"You could say that," Beth chuckled. "She lives just down the street from me. Completely ignores me now if I ever see her outside. But anyway, thanks for asking the follow-up question at the meeting."

"Oh God. They take it so seriously, don't they?" Chloe commiserated. "It's like their little fiefdom and when you rattle their cage they just get all bent out of shape."

They chatted some more. Chloe, and her husband, it turned out, were much more tuned in to local politics than Beth. Chloe told her how a small clique pretty much ran all the boards and committees in the town, and that the mastermind behind the operation was Jim Mortensen. Chloe clearly held him in the utmost contempt. She said that there were also a bunch of what she called "hangers on" who were all desperate to gain some standing in the clique.

"Pam's one of them." She laughed "People like her just can't wait to get into a position where they can make decisions for you and me – whether we want her to or not. Mortensen makes them pay their dues first though. It'll be a while before Pam gets elected to anything."

It was a surprise to Beth to hear someone suggest that there was this pseudo political party at work in her town. It sounded almost a bit Mafioso.

"If they've got so much clout, then why don't they do something about the schools?" asked Beth "Surely they can see as well as we can that lots of the kids are achieving far less than they could in the classrooms?"

Chloe laughed again.

"Oh, please!" she said " That's the farthest thing from their minds! The real players, like Mortensen, all have their kids in private school anyway."

"It sounded as if Pam didn't approve of private schools. If so, why does she hang with those guys?" asked Beth.

"Oh! They can overlook almost anything amongst their own group. It's 'Do as I say not as I do'. Same with the teachers, loads of them send their kids to private schools then go and lobby the government to try and stop other folks, who can't afford it without assistance, from doing the same thing."

Chloe had obviously researched the voucher issue. She had found out that in California, for example, public school teachers sent their own children to private schools at three times the rate of the general population. Yet their protests against school choice initiatives were backed with tens of millions of dollars from the coffers of their own unions. When a state representative had proposed legislation in Sacramento that public school teachers should be prohibited from educating their children privately, the teachers had nevertheless howled that the bill violated their rights. The legislation died promptly.

"What do the teachers think of Mortensen and his team?" Beth asked.

"Well," replied Chloe. "It's just one big mutual admiration society. Sickening really. It works like this. Mortensen's a control freak – just has to be the one making all the decisions or he's not happy. Years ago, when he arrived in Sunbury, he figured out that the way to build a political machine was to ingratiate himself to the public administrators and the unions. The previous group loved all the power too, but at least they weren't in the pockets of the unions."

"So how did he get to be in charge?" asked Beth.

"Easy. He went to the union chiefs and let them know that if he was running the show, they'd do much better when it came to contract negotiations. Not just that, he promised he'd get them lots of nice new buildings too. Then he got a few friends to put their names down as candidates for the town council and school board. Those two boards control all of the money. The union people came out in force, putting up signs, letters to the editor all that sort of thing. Demonized the other side. It doesn't take a lot to win a local election if your opponent isn't really expecting a challenge."

"And what about the administrators? The principals and the superintendent?"

"They're like pigs at the trough. Anytime they think there may be more money coming their way, with less strings attached, they jump on board. Mortensen promised them he wouldn't make a fuss over the lousy test scores and that was all they needed to hear."

"So who speaks up for families and students?" Beth asked with growing exasperation.

"Take a look in the mirror," laughed Chloe. "Nobody else is going to lift a finger on behalf of your kids. It's not just our town, the same thing happens everywhere."

"But shouldn't the board be acting for us, as customers of the system?" Beth persisted. It was hard for her to think of an entire system which seemed to function more for the benefit of the providers of service than for the consumers. It didn't seem very American somehow.

"Absolutely," Chloe confirmed. "In the perfect world, the board, the administrators and the teachers should be at each other's throats. The board should be demanding all sorts of performance improvements if the administrators want to keep their jobs. And the administrators, in turn, should be demanding more of the teachers if they want to keep theirs. But that's not what happens. The whole lot of them, put together, have been called 'The Blob' because they're just one great immovable obstruction to progress."

"Why don't more people complain?" Beth wanted to know.

"Propaganda."

"What?!"

"Propaganda. Pure and simple. They just keep telling all of the parents how lucky the town is to have such a quality school system, and how it would be even better if the voters would just approve one more new building. Of course, that never makes it any better because buildings don't teach math."

Chloe was warming to the task. She continued, "Of course, the real kicker is that they control the grading. It's laughable really, all they have to do is write enough "A"s on the report cards and it stifles nearly all dissent. We parents are a funny lot. We're so desperate for our children to be perceived as brilliant that whenever someone tells us so, we believe them without question. We all think it reflects on us. If the kids are brilliant, then we must be brilliant for having bred them. It's hard not to fall into that trap – do it myself sometimes."

"So, in other words as long as we can say our kids are getting a good education, nobody ever looks too deeply into whether it's actually true or not." Beth was catching on.

"Exactly. It's all appearance."

"Is that why Pam got so snotty when I asked her about the test scores?"

"Of course." Chloe went on. "They hate outside testing more than anything else because they can't fake the results. When they put seventy percent of the kids on the honor roll, but then only ten percent can score 'Proficient' on an externally graded test it makes them look stupid. So they discredit the test. They say it's unfair, discriminates against minorities, even though we don't have any, and so on. After a while, they lobby the State Board of Education to change the scoring mechanism so that they can say the kids did better – even though they didn't."

"And they get away with it?" Beth asked.

"Every time," answered Chloe. "You know, other countries don't allow teachers to grade their own students on exams that are going to be used for college admissions. They have separate examining boards. I was talking to a family from France once and describing our system. They couldn't believe it. They asked me why the teachers didn't just give "A"s to everyone so that the school would look good. I had to admit that as long as you showed up, that's pretty much what happens. There are some dreadful dunces in the high school carrying GPA's of 4.0."

"Apparently, in Europe, the kids never badger teachers for grades because what the teacher says doesn't count for anything. The only thing that matters is what the independent external examiner says. So the teacher's an ally, and the examiner, who's anonymous, is the adversary. It must make for a very different classroom atmosphere if you think about it."

Beth did think about it. It made a lot of sense.

"The problem with our system," Chloe went on, "is that it's self perpetuating. Suppose you get a new teacher who has some academic integrity and starts handing out "D"s and "F"'s. The parents go berserk. It's ironic that the only way you can get

60

them involved is to tell them the truth. They conclude the teacher must be lousy, when, in fact, she might be the only good one in the place. Everything's back to front."

"What happens then?"

"The principal has a quiet word with the offending teacher who is made to realize that she's rocking the boat. If she doesn't jack the grades, then she's going to be looking for other employment next year. Of course, they don't say that in so many words, or put anything in writing, but that's the message."

Beth was silent for a moment. She thought back to her own school days. Of course, even then she had known where to go for an easy "A". But it wasn't all like that. It sounded as though grade inflation was now just completely out of control.

It was hardly surprising really. There was nothing to keep it in check other than the teacher's integrity. And it seemed as if that wasn't easy to maintain – if you wanted a job! It was in everyone's interest in 'The Blob" to just keep on doling out "A"'s. The teachers looked good, the principal looked good, the parents were happy, the board got re-elected, the teachers got better raises.

She shook her head. The only group in the entire picture who were getting royally screwed were the kids themselves. It was happening at the precise moment in the country's history when they needed high level academic skills more than ever before. And they were the only ones who could not fight back. It was hardly reasonable to expect a fifteen year old to pry himself away from the TV to go along to a board meeting and say, "I need more homework, and, by the way, I expect a bad grade if I get the wrong answers."

But what of the colleges? Where did they fit into all of this? Lots of the kids were still managing to gain admittance.

"Yes," agreed Chloe, "but think about it. If you're a college, you have to fill the seats in order to generate revenue. If the overall bell curve of student performance in high school declines, and you maintain your position in the academic hierarchy of all the colleges, then you have to lower your standards to keep the same enrollment. That's why whenever you open the paper you can find an article with some college professor complaining that the kids can't write anymore – and even if they could, they don't know any facts to write about. Of course, then the profs get told to shut up too because the college presidents don't want the image of their school damaged either. Bad for business."

"Do you think that's really the case?" Beth was flabbergasted. American colleges were supposed to be the best in the world. Was that just propaganda too?

"You bet!" yelled Chloe. "They have remedial reading classes at most colleges these days. Oh sure, there are some clever kids getting in to the Ivy League, but the only requirement for most of the rest is that you're breathing and your Dad can afford the fees. After that it's: 'Come on down'."

Beth's head was swimming. She felt as if her world had been turned upside down. Nothing was what it appeared to be.

"Chloe," she said. "What do you think of school choice vouchers?"

"Oh God!" exclaimed Chloe, "Don't get me started. Of course we should have vouchers! But if you want to get your head ripped off in public, proposing vouchers is about the easiest way to achieve it. If there's one thing this crew hates, it's the suggestion that their precious monopoly on the money be taken away from them."

Beth decided she needed to learn more about these voucher things which seemed so sensible yet got everybody so worked up.

CHAPTER 10
"The child is not the mere creature of the state"
US Supreme Court in Pierce v Society of Sisters

When the boys who had stormed the beaches of Normandy, or fought their way up Mount Suribachi, came home from World War II, an understandably grateful nation launched the GI bill to help them out with the funding they would need for a college education.

The bill provided the funds, but the students made the decisions about which colleges they would like to attend.

Many of them took the grants and used them at fine institutions of learning, such as Boston College or Notre Dame, that had a decidedly religious flavor.

Everyone thought it was marvelous.

There was a very different reaction, however, whenever the same sort of thing was proposed in more recent times in K – 12 education. For instance if anyone suggested that the local catholic school might do a better, and much cheaper, job of educating some students, almost immediately all the supporters of the status quo in public schools started yelling "separation of church and state".

Beth decided she wanted to know where this insistence on separation had come from, and why it seemed to be much more seriously adhered to in some situations than in others.

She wasn't a religious person. She didn't have anything against religion. She just chose not to practice it herself. But she could see that there had obviously been a huge step taken to get to the point where today religion was so unwelcome in some, but not all, government funded educational programs.

In particular, was it really cut and dried constitutionally, that families could not use public money to send children to private schools, whether or not the receiving schools were religious? It seemed very strange to her that the law would embrace the concept for colleges, but not for primary and secondary education.

Her first port of call in her research was the text of the United States Constitution. She hit "control-F" on her computer to scan the text she had downloaded. But when she entered "separation of church and state" and clicked on the "search" button, all that came back was a message: "Text not found".

Many Americans, she thought, would be surprised by the fact that this phrase does not appear anywhere in the nation's fundamental document of law.

As she studied further, she found that the words had probably originated with Thomas Jefferson, not in any of the documents that form the title deeds of the country, but instead in a letter that he wrote to the Danbury Baptist Association of Connecticut at the beginning of 1802. The association had written to him offering congratulations on his election as President. In response, and probably knowing how much the Baptists disliked church state entanglement, Jefferson told them that he saw the First Amendment as acting like "a wall of separation". Little did he realize that what may have been an off the cuff remark, one aimed at building his popularity in a part of the country that did not generally lean his way politically, would have such deep and long lasting impact.

Beth thought that in an era when religion was, almost everywhere, more ingrained into daily life than it is today, it would be hard to conclude that the objectives of the framers of the Constitution and Bill of Rights were really to remove religion entirely from the town square.

She looked at the wording of the First Amendment: "Congress shall make no law respecting an establishment of religion, or prohibiting the free exercise thereof..". When it talked about "establishment", what that had meant to the Founders was not that there should be no religion, but that there should be no official state religion, or established church, like the Church of England.

The more she read the first two clauses, known as the "establishment" clause and the "free exercise clause" the more she realized it was one of those "rights of your fist end at the tip of my nose" situations. If the establishment clause was interpreted in a very broad way, so as to keep religion out of every aspect of public life, then it could infringe on someone's free exercise. For example, if a court were to rule that it was not constitutional to say a Christian prayer at the inauguration of a new President, lest it be perceived as state promotion of that particular religion, then the President might say that his rights of free exercise were being infringed.

Later she learned that this was known in legal circles as "the play in the joints" of the first amendment, and that much of first amendment law related to precisely where the line should be drawn between these two competing interests in a huge variety of different situations.

Actually, the lines tended to be drawn wherever the political inclinations of a majority of the Supreme Court justices lay at any particular time, and so the legal no-man's land between "the joints" became, over time, an incomprehensible tangle of often contradictory precedent.

In the gentlemanly tradition of the Court, the principle of "stare decisis", or "to stand by the decision", was, of practical necessity, paramount. What "stare decisis" meant was that the court would consider itself bound by precedent.

Beth had realized, very early in her study, that the idealized notion of a politically neutral Supreme Court, deciding cases on merit and the wording of the Constitution, was nothing more than a myth. The Court was every bit as political as the other branches of government, with the added benefit for justices that, as lifetime appointees, they never had to answer to the electorate for their decisions.

Fortunately, everybody recognized that it was not practical, every time the political leanings of the court majority flip-flopped, simply to undo all previous decisions and start over. Instead, new majorities looked for loopholes in previous decisions that would enable them to nudge a particular boundary in their favored direction. It was death by a thousand cuts. Often a particular justice, or coalition of several justices, would spend decades, and a whole line of cases, in writing opinions which, collectively, established a new way of looking at a particular issue.

It took a truly momentous set of events to overturn entirely a prior Supreme Court decision. Beth would discover that no such violent upheaval had occurred in regard to voucher laws. Instead, the second half of the twentieth century had seen, slowly but surely, several decisions that put together a legal framework of understanding of the situation. In combination, they provided a reality that was actually quite different to the knee-jerk and dogmatic "vouchers are not constitutional" that was heard so often from the uninformed.

Another player who had had a major impact on the development of the law as it pertained to school choice was Senator James G. Blaine, Republican of Maine.

Blaine was hardly a household name in modern times. Beth had never heard of him, and, because of that, was surprised to learn of the degree of his political influence in the reconstruction period following the civil war. Blaine had been a Congressman, Speaker of the House of Representatives, a Senator, and was twice Secretary of State. In 1884 he had been the Republican nominee for President.

For much of the later part of the nineteenth century, in fact, Blaine, rather dramatically known as "the Plumed Knight", had been the figurehead of the Republican party. In an attempt to unite the party in advance of the 1876 elections, Blaine sought to capitalize on widespread anti-Catholic sentiment that had emerged in response to huge waves of Irish and Italian immigration.

He allowed his name to be associated with a proposed constitutional amendment that he, personally, had not authored. Since his mother was Catholic, it is also quite likely that he had little personal sympathy with the goals of the proposal.

The amendment, in an era when daily readings from the King James Bible were the accepted norm in the publicly supported "common schools" across the country, would have prohibited public money from flowing to any "religious" school. "Religious" in this sense meant anything not Protestant!

The so-called "Blaine Amendment" failed to garner the necessary votes in Congress to be submitted to the states for ratification to the United States Constitution. However, undeterred, the supporters of the amendment fanned out across the country and, over the years, managed to insert similar language into no less than thirty-seven state constitutions.

Given that the "Blaine's", as the state amendments became known, were so firmly rooted in religious xenophobia and bigotry, several of the commentaries that Beth read considered them to be embarrassing stains on documents intended to frame the highest ideals of societal structure.

Taken together, the state Blaine amendments, and the notion of the "wall of separation", would provide the foundations that enterprising lawyers would use to attempt to construct a legalistic and financial Berlin Wall around the monopoly of the nation's public schools.

As Beth was discovering, school district employees, administrators and officials all stood guard on the ramparts of this citadel. Interestingly, they were facing inwards, preventing escape. Only the wealthy could buy their way out to the greener educational fields, represented by the more successful private schools on the other side of the wall.

Blaine and Jefferson, she thought, would probably both have been horrified to learn the degree to which their actions, through the Law of Unintended Consequences, had resulted in the total banishment of all forms of religious expression from modern classrooms.

Jefferson's "wall of separation" phrase, largely forgotten for almost one hundred and fifty years, next reared its head in the Supreme Court's opinion in the case of *Everson v Board of Education* in 1947.

The *Everson* case was brought by a New Jersey taxpayer who objected to the fact that local school districts were using public funds to reimburse parents for bus fares for transporting students to and from private schools, the vast majority of which were Catholic schools. He claimed that this practice violated the first amendment by providing aid to religious schools.

The majority opinion, in a 5-4 decision, was authored by Justice Hugo Black. Black was an FDR appointee, who, earlier in his life had joined the Ku Klux Klan in the hope that it would advance his political career in Alabama.

"God," Beth thought. "There were obviously no limits back then either!"

The opinion was a curious one. Everson actually lost his case, with Black writing that such transportation was not prohibited by the First Amendment. He likened the situation of spending money on transportation to religious schools to local spending on police and firemen, pointing out that emergency services did not discriminate against religious establishments in protecting citizens from crime or fires that might occur on those premises.

He suggested a couple of important principles. Firstly that transportation to school was actually a general benefit afforded to all families, and as such, did not represent any particular aid to religious schools. And secondly, that the issue was clouded by the fact that no public money actually flowed directly to religious schools, in that it was reimbursed to parents.

So Black drew his line between the joints on the basis of the service offered, and the path taken by the money.

It was however, the other more general remarks about aid to religious schools, which had a decidedly different tone.

For at the end of his opinion Black wrote:

"The State contributes no money to the schools. It does not support them. Its legislation, as applied, does no more than provide a general program to help parents get their children, regardless of their religion, safely and expeditiously to and from accredited schools.

The First Amendment has erected a wall between church and state. That wall must be kept high and impregnable. We could not approve the slightest breach. New Jersey has not breached it here."

Mr. Everson, therefore, cannot have been too disappointed in his loss. While Justice Black had said there was nothing wrong with a few public pennies of bus fare being used to get a student to a Catholic school, he had put the much larger and more meaningful issue of tuition costs firmly out of bounds for a long time.

Constitutional law, as Beth was discovering, moves along at a funereal pace. Years, and even decades, can go by without a suitable case coming before the Court which can be used to revisit and refine a prior decision.

And so it was with school choice. Nothing much happened for a quarter of a century until the *Nyquist* case arrived. And even that didn't help matters much!

The *Nyquist* case, heard in 1973, related to a proposal for direct public financial support of parochial schools in New York. The proposal was brought about by the financial difficulties and widespread closure of parochial schools, and the resultant over-enrollment in the public system. New York's argument was that it was much cheaper to prop up the Catholic schools financially than to absorb all of the displaced students into the public system.

Once again, as in *Everson*, the *Nyquist* opinion had two seemingly opposite outcomes. The aid program was struck down since the court concluded that the "primary effect" of the program was to advance religion. However, now on the bench was the relatively recently appointed Justice William Rehnquist, destined to become the Chief Justice in 1986. While agreeing to the main point, but writing separately in dissent, Rehnquist concluded that the decision importantly left open the question of whether, in future, a case:

"involving some form of public assistance (e.g. scholarships) made available generally without regard to the sectarian-non sectarian or public non-public nature of the institution benefited"

might pass constitutional muster.

By emphasizing the notion of an "indirect" benefit, Rehnquist had found the route around Black's "wall of separation" without having to upset protocol by dynamiting the thing and thereby disturbing the existing precedent. What he was saying, in effect, was that while he agreed it was unconstitutional for the government to send money directly to religious schools, if the money was instead given to the parents who could send it wherever they wished, then the situation was entirely different. In that eventuality, the benefit accrued to the parent not the school. If eventually some of the money arrived at a local Catholic school as a result of the parent's subsequent choices, then it was really no different than the accepted situation of someone drawing unemployment benefits and putting money into a church collection plate.

Rehnquist was arguing that government money ceases to become public money at the point that it is dispensed, and that there are limits to the restrictions that government can place on the disposition of that money. It is as if the existence of a parent, redirecting the money to the school of their choice, acts as a circuit breaker between church and state.

Nyquist can be considered a turning point. It settled the matter of direct aid once and for all, but it ushered in a long era of decisions pertaining to indirect aid.

Over the next thirty years a number of cases came to the court that picked around the edges of the issue.

Mueller, in 1983, involved a Minnesota statute that provided tax deductions for educational expenses, including private school tuition. The majority upheld the tax deductions because the beneficiaries had a realistic choice between religious and non-religious options. Aid was transferred to religious institutions only as a result of such choice. *Mueller* set a precedent in suggesting that public dollars are constitutionally "laundered" by the process of choice.

Aguilar, in 1985 established that students at religious schools were entitled to receive remedial services from public school teachers under the federal Title 1 program, but that the services could not occur on religious school premises. The decision led to trailers being parked in the yards of religious schools. Later, in *Agostini* in 1997, a different majority removed the restriction on the use of religious school premises.

In *Witters* in 1986, the Court unanimously upheld the use of college aid by a blind student from Washington studying for the ministry at a school of divinity. The decision followed Mueller in stressing that the aid program itself was not religious since the recipient had a wide variety of choices available to him.

The *Zobrest* case in 1993 upheld a program that provided a publicly funded interpreter for a deaf student attending a Catholic High School. The interpreter provided signing during both secular and religious classes.

Mitchell in 2000 allowed a program in Louisiana, that delivered computers and software, to include private and parochial schools. The decision rested on the "neutrality" of the program.

Beth, who had never previously found the law all that interesting, was becoming fascinated by the process. She recognized that a few days of reading hardly qualified her as an expert on the subject, but she thought she could detect Rehnquist's fingerprints and leadership on all of these decisions. Here was this one man, working away slowly but so surely in a single direction over all this time. Nudging along a project, often having to wait years between opportunities for taking the next step.

She wondered what Rehnquist must have thought when the case of *Zelman v Simmons-Harris* arrived on the Supreme Court docket in 2002.

Zelman was a direct test of whether the precedent that Rehnquist had so painstakingly built over so many years would stand up to the onslaught of the ultimate question: "Could public money be used indirectly, as a result of parental choice, to pay tuition, not just incidentals like transportation or books, at private and religious schools."

The State of Ohio had enacted a voucher program several years previously in response to the truly awful conditions and results of the Cleveland Public School system. Several thousand students had been able to avail themselves of the program, and were enrolled in private schools with the fees being paid by public money dispersed to parents in the form of certificates that could be made over to schools. Because it was mainly Catholic schools that had tuition fees sufficiently low to be covered by the value of the voucher, the vast majority of voucher recipients were attending these schools.

As usual, the teachers unions and administrators were livid about the loss of their monopoly, particularly because it was glaringly apparent that almost none of the voucher students were in any hurry whatsoever to return to the public system after once tasting the forbidden fruit of private education.

So they brought suit against the program on First Amendment establishment clause grounds.

It was interesting, Beth thought, that it was always the providers of educational services, and never the consumers, that objected to vouchers, even when it was shown that the outcomes were favorable for the voucher students. The same teachers who normally liked to represent themselves as selfless facilitators, whose only concern was the best interests of their students, were quite happy to fight tooth and nail to return voucher students to less advantageous surroundings.

After several years of winding its way through lower courts, the Ohio case duly arrived at the Supreme Court where it was widely believed that Justice Sandra Day O'Connor would represent the swing vote. Choice supporters heaved a collective sigh of relief when, during the oral arguments, O'Connor asked a question that indicated that she had bought into the concept that if parents had a genuine choice, in other words if religious schools were not the only option, then the public money that was given to them was sufficiently disconnected from the government by the time that it reached the schools to avoid any infringement of the establishment clause.

When the opinion was finally read several months later on the last day of the Court's session in the summer of 2003, it was Chief Justice Rehnquist himself who had authored the decision. In allowing the program to continue, he summed up his work over the previous thirty years, thus:

" *..our decisions have drawn a consistent distinction between government programs that provide aid directly to religious schools...and programs of true private choice,* *in which government aid reaches religious schools only as a result of the genuine and independent choices of private individuals…"*

Beth sensed it must have been a moment of high intellectual triumph for Rehnquist, who had maneuvered his way through the "play in the joints" for three decades to finally see the concept of indirect payments become firmly ensconced as "stare decisis".

Zelman v Simmons Harris was surely a crushing defeat for the public education lobby.

Most people in the United States would think that once the Supreme Court had spoken in such a fashion the game was up for the opponents.

However, the teachers were not going to give up easily. They licked their wounds, and cheered up considerably when their lawyers told them that although the outer walls of their monopoly had been breached, they still had a sturdy second line of defense, provided for them a long time ago by Senator James Blaine.

Of course the lawyers were happy too because it meant that the gravy train of taxpayer money which flowed from the teachers' paychecks to the union to the lawyers' fees was not going to be drying up anytime soon.

"Oh no!" thought Beth. "This just keeps getting worse. When we pay our property taxes we're actually forking some of it over to pay for lawyers to trap our own kids in schools that don't work."

Senator Blaine, or at least the supporters of the amendment named after him, had thrown a monkey wrench into "the play in the joints" that even Rehnquist was not able to untangle before he died.

The language of the First Amendment in the United States Constitution is much less specific than the language of the Blaine amendments that now defile so many state constitutions. The Blaine amendments clearly state that public money cannot go to religious schools. The reason that it was from Ohio that a case like *Zelman* had originated was fairly straightforward. Ohio is one of the states that does not have a Blaine Amendment.

So, after *Zelman*, voucher opponents simply regrouped and started attacking voucher proposals at the state level on Blaine Amendment grounds.

The more she read, the more it struck Beth that there was something truly bizarre about the motives and methods of the voucher opponents. The major problem with the nation's public schools, it seemed to her, was that they had abandoned the pursuit of knowledge and learning, and instead had become factories indoctrinating values on to impressionable young minds. Among these values, she had heard school personnel preach over and over again, were tolerance and respect for diversity of opinion.

Yet here were the same people, in attempting to defend their monopoly, using as a shield the legacy of one of the most blatantly bigoted episodes in the entire pantheon of American history! She suspected that many of them didn't even know that.

In a state where a Blaine amendment existed, and New Hampshire was one such state, the problems for voucher supporters were enormous. First of all, they had to convince both houses of a state congress, and a governor that the idea was a good one. This in and of itself, represented a daunting task since the teachers union contributed so massively to the political war chests of politicians.

If a proposal made it as far as state law, a legal challenge was inevitable from the monopolists, and voucher supporters would have to persuade a state Supreme Court that even the Blaine amendment with its specific language, should be subject to the *Zelman* principle that indirect payments are different from direct aid.

In New Hampshire, Beth learned, the political make-up of the Supreme Court made it almost impossible that such an argument would succeed.

Beyond that, there would only be one appeal and that would be to the United States Supreme Court. The appeal there would be different from the *Zelman* case. *Zelman* was an establishment clause case, with the plaintiffs challenging an existing voucher program on the grounds that it represented aid to religion.

In the case that Beth was envisioning the appeal would be from the free exercise side of "the play in the joints". The argument would be that in applying a strict interpretation of the Blaine Amendment in the State Constitution, and saying that no money could go to religious schools even indirectly, the state court had crossed over the boundary, and was now infringing on the free exercise rights guaranteed in the United States Constitution. In effect the argument would be that the Blaine Amendments themselves are unconstitutional.

For the last couple of years, since the appointments of John Roberts and Samuel Alito, there had been five Catholics on the nine member United States Supreme Court. In that time however, no cases of significance to school choice had come before the court. It was thought, in legal circles, that Justices Scalia and Thomas might have some sympathy for denying such a broad application of the Blaines, and there was some hope among voucher supporters that Roberts and Alito might vote that way also if push came to shove. But there was a lot of doubt about Justice Anthony Kennedy and absolutely no chance that any of Stevens, Souter, Ginsberg or Breyer, all of whom had dissented in *Zelman*, would take the even greater step of reining in the Blaine Amendments.

Without a reliable majority, it was unlikely that the supportive justices would even vote to take such a case on to the Supreme Court docket.

"My goodness. A long road to hoe," thought Beth.

How tragic it seemed, that just when the nation was at its most vulnerable, performing poorly in competing with the new players in the global economy, not just political but also a host of legal obstacles were placed in the way of the one thing that stood a chance of rescuing the situation.

CHAPTER 11

"Globalization has changed us into a company that searches the world, not just to sell or to source, but to find intellectual capital - the world's best talents and greatest ideas."

Jack Welch, Chairman of General Electric

OCTOBER 2008

BANGALORE, INDIA

Around about the same time that Beth Southwick had been at the parents' evening, on the other side of the world, eight thousand miles to the east and ten hours ahead of her, a young man named Arunkhumar Patel was just getting up in his small but tidy apartment in Bangalore. While Beth was listening to her child's teachers explain all the sophisticated theories for why American children should not accelerate their learning program, Arunkhumar Patel was putting into practice all the reasons why they should.

Patel's educational experience as a young man had been very different from the one that was presented to the children of Sunbury. Nobody had ever felt particularly concerned about his self esteem, but his family and teachers had definitely exhibited an interest in making sure that he approached his studies with sufficient diligence. He could still remember the times when, from the age of about eight onwards, he would have to hold out his arms to be whipped by his father whenever he did poorly on a math test. He wouldn't wish that treatment on anyone, but could not deny that it had certainly provided a motivation to do better the next time.

Outside of his front door, and down the street, all of the chaos, the grime and the beggars of India were readily apparent. But the fiber optic cables made their way unscathed through all that and provided him with a broadband internet connection that was every bit as efficient at allowing him to communicate with the rest of the world as if he were sitting in the Rockefeller Center in New York City.

Patel, armed as a result of his stern upbringing with a significant capability in mathematics, had moved on to the University of Bangalore, where he had studied Finance and Information Technology. He had actually lived in New York for a couple of years. He was a recipient of one of the so-called H1-B visas.

The United States was not only a place where free markets in raw materials and manufactured goods thrived, but also one where there were relatively few restrictions on the movement of people who could provide valuable labor.

The H1-B visa program had been created to address a specific perceived shortage in the availability of technology workers. Whether there was a real shortage, or whether the captains of industry had pressured the politicians for the program so that an influx of lower wage graduates from overseas would depress the salaries of domestic employees, was the subject of heated argument.

Nevertheless each year, tens of thousands of qualified software engineers and other technical operators arrived in the United States for stays of several years that were allowed by the visa program. A large proportion of H1-B recipients were Asian, particularly Indians.

The Indian post secondary education system, although only open to a far smaller percentage of the population than in the United States, produced a large number of well qualified engineers. Even at salaries that were substantially lower than those offered to domestic employees, American incomes offered to H1-B recipients appeared like a king's ransom to young Indian graduates. Hardly surprising when the GDP in India only amounted to less than a thousand dollars per capita per year.

With the frugality built into their psyche from a lifetime of shortages, they lived inexpensively and either sent home what appeared like truckloads of rupees to grateful relatives, or stashed the proceeds away looking forward to a day when those funds would buy them an exceptionally comfortable lifestyle back home.

Over time, many, seduced by the bright lights, the swimming pools and airplanes, and the conspicuous consumption endemic to an American lifestyle, managed to convert their temporary visas into green cards and settled permanently. But for others, living in a foreign culture, however glitzy and comfortable, was still quite definitely not like being at home.

Arunkhumar was one such. He had been lonely a lot of the time, spending many evenings on his own cycling endlessly through the channels on his TV. Adrift and alone, he returned to his family in India after the completion of his initial contract.

The time that he had spent in America, though, had opened his eyes to the colossal discrepancy in incomes and living costs between India and America. Returning to India and converting the money he had saved in the United States back into Indian rupees, he realized that he could afford to live quite comfortably for a couple of years without an income. He was sure that somewhere in the financial divide between what he had seen in America, and what existed outside his door, there was a major business opportunity, and he was going to try and find it.

He was fully aware of the extraordinary Indian success stories of companies like Wipro, Infosys and Tata that had made fortunes by delivering technical services to the Western world, charging something close to Western prices while paying their employees Asian salaries. Wipro had been begun in a garage only about twenty years ago. Patel was twenty-five years old. If he could realize even a fraction of that success he would still be in his prime when he could retire to a life of fabulous wealth and privilege.

He had spent some time considering offering online tutoring services. There were a number of companies expanding rapidly into the field of helping American kids to do their homework via the internet. It was a neat idea really, there were millions of students in the United States who would quite happily trade a few bucks for the right answers to their worksheets, or some test preparation help. And there were many, many young men and women in Bangalore who, with upbringings similar to Patel's had the skills necessary to provide assistance.

He had even taken a job for a while, just to research the occupation, at a place that offered college essay writing services. Bailey Hutchins. That name stuck in his head. How many times had he rewritten that guy's paper for a single fee. There had to be better rates of return in other business ventures. Besides, call center work was already starting to become unfashionable. He continued his search.

The business model he had eventually seized upon was based on the phenomenal price advantage that India enjoyed over the United States in the delivery of medical care.

On his computer that morning, he was putting the finishing touches to the business plan that he would soon start offering to the venture capital firms. His goal was to provide a one stop shopping experience for medical patients seeking cheaper treatment in India.

A surgical procedure and post operative care that might cost $100,000 in the United States could be obtained for perhaps $20,000 in the best hospitals in India utilizing entirely US trained doctors. Even allowing for recuperation periods in five star hotels and first class round trip airfare it would still cost far less than half as much as comparable care in the US.

Arunkhumar had learned that many large United States corporations were self insuring in regard to employee health care. A deal like this just had to look good to them. They would even be able to offer their employees a meaningful amount of the savings as a cash bonus to provide them with the incentive to travel overseas for procedures.

Furthermore, it would look good to thousands of people living with constant pain in Western democracies where socialized medicine programs had resulted in enormous waiting lists for procedures like hip replacements.

Young Patel envisioned a scenario where, like a package holiday operator, he would put together the entire program of medical treatment, transportation and recuperation accommodation. Of course, some little golden crumbs of commission would fall off each service provider's take on each transaction, right into the lap of Arunkhumar Patel.

There was, of course, no guarantee that any new business plan would eventually receive the approval and support of funding sources. But Patel was not alone. Across the city of Bangalore, across India, and indeed across Asia and the rest of the third world, capable young men in a hurry, just like him, were putting together their plans to help themselves to a piece of the global financial pie. It was a pie that until recently had saved its best slices for Americans.

But while America busied itself with plans to stop its first graders from reading and calculating, Arunkhumar Patel and his peers were intent on demonstrating that it was not just in the manufacture of jeans and laptop computers that reserved slices of pie were about to become a thing of the past.

CHAPTER 12
"However beautiful the strategy, you should occasionally look at the results."
Winston Churchill, British Politician and Prime Minister

OCTOBER 2008

SCHOOL BOARD MEETING ROOM, SUNBURY, NEW HAMPSHIRE

Jim Mortensen reclined in his chair at the apex of the horseshoe shaped table and surveyed the scene. His outward appearance was serious and barely tolerant, as though he believed that he was burdened by some huge service that only his massive intellect could encompass, and for which he was not adequately recognized or respected. In reality, though, he was exactly where he wanted to be.

As chairman, he liked to get to board meetings a few minutes before everyone else and watch the small crowd build. Typically, meetings were attended by the five board members, the school district superintendent and a couple of his staff members. They all sat at the table. Folding chairs were laid out sufficient to accommodate an audience of around thirty. They were rarely filled. The usual suspects began to file in. A couple of the principals from the five schools that constituted the district; a teachers' union representative; an old duffer who considered himself the town sage, but in reality had nothing better to do with his time than go to all the local board meetings; the beat reporter from the local rag; some guy from the taxpayer's association. Parents of students almost never attended - unless they were after money to start up a new sport.

"All those A's on the report cards," thought Mortensen.

He had the Superintendent to thank for the administration of that important little task.

Superintendent Hamlin walked in and took his seat three places to the left of Mortensen. They gave each other a perfunctory nod. There was no particular friendship there, for theirs was a working relationship. They each recognized their need for the support of the other. The superintendent of the school district was the only employee who reported to the board. All other district employees reported either directly or indirectly to him.

And so the annual elections of school board members were of particular interest to the superintendent. The board comprised five members, each serving three year terms. So in the normal way of things, there would be two seats up for grabs two years out of every three, and one seat in the other year. The political complexion of the board, and consequently what its majority expected of its superintendent, could therefore change by one hundred and eighty degrees at a single election.

Fortunately for Hamlin, for his entire tenure as superintendent, there had been no flies in the ointment. No new crusading board members out for dramatic reform of either district spending, or, his worst nightmare, student performance. As long as

Mortensen held all the political cards in Sunbury, Hamlin's position was relatively safe.

Miles Hamlin knew that with Mortensen in place, nobody would get a chance to delve too deeply into his contract details or ask awkward questions about how he was hording deferred income for untaken vacation and unused sick days. One day, his exit strategy would pay off when all that extra income would be lumped into his final year's salary, dramatically boosting the basis on which his lifetime pension would be calculated. In return he would make sure those A's kept flowing.

Mortensen focused on the documents in the packet in front of him, but glanced up as each attendee entered the room. Years of political involvement had provided him with an unerring capability to read people's intentions through their eyes and body language. Were they here to attack or to compliment? Were they offering to volunteer or looking for a financial hand-out. Most importantly of all, did they have that determined, superior look that signified they might harbor hostile political ambitions.

Not that any level of determination would do them much good in that regard. Mortensen had spent years putting together his political machine. He decided who got elected in this town. Period.

His mind wandered back over the past decade. The titanic struggle to dislodge the previous crew who ran the place. The alliances he had managed to forge with the public employees unions and the administrators. The promises he had made to the police, the firefighters and the school principals about how he would battle for salary increases and new facilities for them. The political support they had so willingly provided in return.

Most of all he looked with satisfaction on his management of the band of loyal followers who constituted his main base. There were perhaps fifty of them with various degrees of involvement.

"What a bunch of dimwits," he thought and chuckled inwardly, but no hint of mirth reached the outside world.

His strategy was simple. Build a hierarchy and populate it with sheep who would never do a thing without asking his permission first, but who would charge over a cliff if he asked them. He maintained their devotion by handing out public awards. Even something as small as a press announcement could almost always be guaranteed to bind another willing adherent to Mortensen's favorite cause: himself.

"Citizen of the Year", however, was the most treasured prize. They all coveted that one, and the press attention that accompanied it. It was officially presented by the Chamber of Commerce, but, since he controlled that group also, it amounted to a political patronage that was his to confer. It was a shame he could only make use of it once each year, the recipients were so grateful.

Mortensen valued loyalty to himself above all else. And it was rewarded with promotions in the hierarchy that were unannounced but clearly understood by all.

Ultimately, when select members of the clan had demonstrated fidelity for several years, and Mortensen was convinced that they didn't possess an original thought in their head to threaten his supremacy one day, he would offer his backing for a run for office.

In Sunbury, a Mortensen backing was tantamount to automatic election. It meant several things. Firstly, nobody else from the clan would run against you and split the vote. In fact, it was quite likely that you would be elected unopposed because most political aspirants in the town understood that to run against Mortensen's candidate was to guarantee a barrage of nasty things about you appearing in the "Letters to the Editor" section of the local paper.

Once campaigns got underway, the anointed clan member was sure of donations from the local chapter of the teachers' union, favorable treatment from local reporters, and an army of supporters hammering in signs. The same supporters could usually be counted upon, after dark, to knock over or burn any signs an opponent tried to put out.

Mortensen himself, of course, was at the pinnacle of the pyramid. Master of All.

"Well," he justified his position to himself. "There hasn't been a community breakfast in ten years where I haven't flipped pancakes for the little brats. That's got to be worth something."

Mortensen's personal opinion of the children who passed through the district's schools was not high. He was glad that his own daughter was at the private Chertsey school, where there was still some discipline and the expectations put on student performance were substantially higher.

He interrupted his reverie as the room filled up. No entrant to the room had looked like a particular threat, and he was anticipating his usual dominance of the proceedings.

"Let's switch on the TV then shall we, and get started," His visage lightened noticeably. Best to present a cheery exterior.

Mortensen was aware that even though very few people came to the meetings, TV viewership was surprisingly high.

One of the principals, anxious to perform a service for the chairman, jumped up and turned the key which would activate the camera and send the images of the meeting down the cable and into the homes of the community. Showtime!

Beth Southwick walked into the room.

Among the little club of regular attendees, Beth's entrance was the cause of considerable interest. They all glanced at her while pretending not to, trying to figure out who she was. Beth caught the quick looks.

"Now I know how a virus feels when the white blood cells are hunting it down," she thought. She felt like an intruder in a secret society.

Jim Mortensen had no idea who Beth was, but she didn't fit any of the usual categories. That made his political antennae twitch. He didn't like the unknown.

He glanced over to Hamlin very quickly to see if he had any read on this unexpected situation. Hamlin, who remembered Beth from the parents' evening, pursed his lips and looked down.

"Trouble," thought Mortensen. Still he was relieved to see that Beth was by herself. Individuals were easier to intimidate than deputations.

He launched into the agenda anyway. Minutes of the previous meeting were approved. There were a handful of resignations and appointments of new teachers.

"Comments from the board?"

None. Check that one off with a flourish. Make a little joke about how well we're doing tonight. Acknowledge ripple of forced laughter from audience. Smile for the camera.

"Superintendent's report?"

"Thank you, Mr. Chairman," Hamlin responded. "There is a matter that I would like to bring to the board's attention." Mortensen already knew that. They spoke to each other a couple of times each day by phone. Hamlin had already run this proposal up the yard arm. Mortensen nodded.

"We have a situation at Sunbury Elementary that I would like the board's guidance on," Hamlin continued.

"There has been an unexpected influx of new students in third grade moving into the district, that has led to our class size there being larger than we would ideally like to be the case."

Duncan Markwell, perched on a chair in the back row, leaned forward. Hamlin was presenting the plan that they had been hatching over the past few weeks.

"We have a proposal from the administrative team at the Elementary to convert the large storage area at the back of the building into an additional classroom. That would give us seven third grade classrooms instead of just six and reduce our expected class size from twenty-two to eighteen or nineteen."

The taxpayer group representative in the audience rolled his eyes, but, seeing no resistance from the board, Hamlin pressed on.

"The estimated investment is expected to be about thirty-five thousand dollars to fit out and equip the room, and then about sixty-five thousand for staff and benefits," he paused for reaction.

"So, a hundred thousand this year, and sixty-five ongoing" Mortensen calculated, without looking up from the pad where he was scribbling the numbers that he already knew from his prior conversations with Hamlin. "Comments from the board?" he asked looking around.

"It just sounds like something we need to do," observed Alice Farmington, seated to his immediate left, using her "concerned" look. "We must remember our commitment to not let class size get outside of the State Board of Education guidelines."

Mortensen already knew that Alice was a "yes" vote, he had talked to each board member individually prior to the meeting.

"Okay, but how do we pay, for it?" asked board vice chair John Reddington, sitting at Mortensen's right.

Reddington was one of Mortensen's favorites. Along with Alice, he was a guaranteed third vote that would assure Mortensen's majority on any issue brought to the board. It had been more than five years since Mortensen's political machine had put up the ticket of Reddington and Alice Farmington for election. In that period Reddington had never once voted against him. Portly and in his fifties, at one level Reddington was an extraordinarily arrogant individual who reveled in the sense of power that public office gave him. At another level though, he feared he was completely inept, and so stuck like glue to Mortensen for political cover.

The question Reddington had asked however was one of Mortensen's favorites. For, along with Hamlin, he shared a secret to which even his inner circle of trusted lieutenants were not privy. The budget was rigged.

Every year when the budget was prepared, union employee salaries made up about half of the total. Health insurance premiums would be at least another ten percent. All union salaries were negotiated on a scale that was reviewed every three years at contract renegotiation. But the structure was always similar. Employees were categorized on a scale that depended firstly on their level of education: bachelors, masters or doctoral degree, and secondly on the number of years of experience.

Each year, every cell in this two dimensional matrix would increase by a negotiated amount, but also each employee would move one step higher up on the experience ranking, effectively giving each of them a double raise.

The sleight of hand that Mortensen enjoyed so much was in the budgeting of this arrangement. In putting together the estimates, the superintendent would budget as if every employee was returning the following year. In other words the entire teaching workforce would move one step higher up the experience ladder. Of course, in reality this was not what happened. Older employees left the district's employ, or retired, and were replaced predominantly by fresh faced recruits from the teacher training schools who began, much less expensively, at the first step of the experience ladder.

The net effect was that the average experience stayed almost exactly the same. Consequently, each year the budget overestimated the average step on the scale by a whole year. Since the step increases were usually about three percent and, and in a sizeable district like Sunbury union salaries amounted to almost thirty million dollars, this little bit of legerdemain put almost a million dollars of cushion into the budget each year. Mortensen regarded it as his own little pot of cash from which he could dispense favors as required during the course of the fiscal year.

Not only that, but in November of each year, when the budgets were being put together for the following school year, the health insurance organizations did not yet have the complete utilization data available on which they would base the following year's premiums. Since they were always anxious not to get caught short themselves in the budgeting process, they could also be counted on to provide an estimate which would nearly always be higher than the actual rate quoted when the premiums were finalized. This often added another one or two hundred thousand to the slush fund from which Mortensen was able to distribute his board largesse.

In most years he would dispense about half to three quarters of the pool of money on all manner of minor requests that came before the board during the course of the year, but which had not been included in the formal budgeting process.

There would be money for new ice hockey uniforms, professional development courses for teachers, trips to "vital" conferences for administrators, upgrades to playing fields and bleachers, and additional hiring and building requests like the ones before him now.

The rest he would roll forward, with great fanfare in the press, as an offset to the following year's local taxation. He would make sure that it was described as "savings" resulting from his prudent and frugal management of the district's finances.

All of these things, he knew, should have rightfully gone in the budget as line items. But the budget had to go before the voters each year, and line items like those generated questions in the press from taxpayers. It was so much more convenient to lump a bit extra into the salaries account and then dole it out with nothing more than a rubberstamp approval from his sidekicks on the board.

And so after Reddington's question, all eyes in the room settled on Mortensen, the self proclaimed financial wizard of Sunbury. Hamlin waited for the question that he knew was coming his way in a couple of moments. Mortensen, pandering to what he perceived as his own flair for the dramatic, peered off into the distance and rubbed his chin.

"There might be some savings in the salaries account that we could use for this, do you think?" he was looking over at Hamlin.

Hamlin looked equally pensive and, after a moment, nodded his assent.

There was a murmur of approval from the crowd. Or at least from the school district employees and board members. They gazed adoringly at their man. Mortensen had come through again in a crunch. What a guy! How lucky Sunbury was to have him! The taxpayer's group representative raised his hand. Mortensen sighed audibly.

"Yes, Bob," he saved the weary tone in his voice especially for moments like this, when some realist might seek to cast doubt and uncertainty on the rabbit that he, The Great Mortensen, had just pulled out of the budgetary hat.

Bob Finn rose to his feet and, following protocol, introduced himself to the meeting.

"Robert Finn, twenty-five Augustine Drive, representing the Sunbury Taxpayer Association."

Beth recognized his name as being that of the writer who had penned the article in the paper about using vouchers to send local children to private schools.

She also detected that the love fest of a couple of moments previously had been replaced by a totally different atmosphere. One of hostility and resentment.

"Jim, you can't just keep on doing things like this. Once again, you're transferring operating funds to capital building projects. Last year you added a baseball field that nobody got to vote on. In the spring, when we were asked to vote on this budget, you told the community it was cut to the bone. Now, just a few weeks after the start of the school year, all of a sudden there's a spare hundred grand just floating around that can be used, apparently, without any other off-setting savings being made?"

The reporter was scribbling madly. Mortensen made a mental note to talk to the editor about how the story would be presented.

"Well, let me stop you right there, Bob," said Mortensen angrily. "Before you get yourself into trouble. The fact is that savings have been made in the hiring that was done over the summer. As usual you've come in here throwing around accusations without any substantiating data."

"Well if you would give us all the data," responded Finn. Beth was impressed. He wasn't backing down at all, and she didn't detect the shake in his voice that had characterized her complaint at the parents' evening. "Then we might have a better idea. But, as usual, the numbers are all one big secret."

"Furthermore," Finn clearly wasn't done. "When you add staff it's supposed to be done through the budget process, and the people get to vote on it, unless an emergency situation exists. I'm having a hard time understanding how anyone could describe class sizes of twenty-two as an emergency."

Mortensen wasn't going to admit anything publicly, but actually, he agreed. But then again, the object of the exercise here was not, in reality, educational in the first place. It was just one more step along the "smaller class size, therefore more teachers continuum" that kept his supporters in the unions happy.

Fortunately for Mortensen, Alice Farmington jumped into the fray.

"Actually, research shows major advantages to class sizes lower than twenty being maintained until after third grade," she was using her haughtiest tone, and the narrowed features, that she reserved especially for situations where she had no idea what she was talking about, but did not want anyone to discover that fact.

"Oh, please! Not the 'research shows' argument again," implored Finn. "You say that every time, but it doesn't take a great deal of research to show that the fortune we've spent on lowering class size in this district over the last decade hasn't improved performance one iota."

Beth noticed, to her distinct surprise, that she was rather enjoying this confrontation. She didn't really know all the rules about who authorized spending, but she sensed that Finn had good information. The board seemed distinctly flustered when confronted with facts.

"And what would you base that detailed analysis on?" challenged Farmington sardonically.

"Easy," snorted Finn. "The average combined SAT was one thousand and twenty a decade ago, and it's still one thousand and twenty today. Tell me where the improvement is."

"SAT scores?" Alice Farmington asked incredulously, as if only an idiot would think that had any bearing on school district performance. She looked around the room, and drew a supportive chuckle from the teachers in attendance.

"That's just one test on one day," Alice went on. "Surely, Mr. Finn, you can't think that that is the only indicator of a successful education program."

"No," replied Finn. "I hope we have some other positive indicators as well. But I find it hard to see how you can claim victory for all this spending when the SAT's haven't improved at all."

Beth remembered how utterly alone she had felt when she had risen to ask her controversial question at the parent's evening. And she recalled the effect on her confidence when Chloe had stood up and asked her supportive question.

Without really intending to, she found herself standing.

Mortensen looked at her, and nodded that she could speak.

"I've heard that the class sizes at George Washington Elementary are smaller," she said, surprised to find that her voice was steadier than the last time she had spoken in public. George Washington was another of the three elementary schools in Sunbury. "Why not let a few of the kids from Sunbury Elementary choose to go there instead of building another classroom."

There was another murmur of disapproval from the district personnel present.

"Could you identify yourself for the record, please," Mortensen used his bored voice to indicate that the suggestion Beth had just made was a complete waste of his valuable time.

"Yes, I'm Beth Southwick, twelve Colonial Drive," she said, and suddenly losing confidence sat back down.

Finn took up the baton.

"Well, I didn't know that," he said. "But what a great idea. Allowing some families to choose to move school if they think the program or class size, or whatever they're looking for, might be better elsewhere. That'll keep everyone on their toes and save us all a whole bunch of money."

Finn had just muttered the educational "C" word, "choose". There was a collective groan from the assembled providers of educational services.

"All right, all right, we're going nowhere with this," interjected Mortensen, banging his gavel to indicate that Finn wasn't going to get to say anything else. "Can I have a motion?"

Just like that, all debate was shut off. Alice made a motion to spend the hundred thousand dollars on the building and staffing, Reddington seconded. There were five quick "Ayes", all in favor, and a major expenditure, never approved by the community's electorate was authorized anyway on their behalf.

"Outrageous," Beth heard Finn mutter under his breath. He turned towards Beth. They hadn't met before but gratitude for her support was implicit in his smile.

The meeting wound on. There was a proposal to resurface the floor in a gymnasium that generated prolonged discussion. Mortensen took a special interest. Despite the fact that the district had a maintenance director on staff who clearly knew far more about floors than all of the board combined, each board member seemed to want to have an input on the type of flooring to be laid down.

Then another forty minutes or more were spent discussing the new elementary school building proposal and the best ways to sell the idea to the community.

Beth sensed a similar pattern emerging to the one she had witnessed at the parent's evening. They seemed to want to talk about everything except the one thing that really mattered which was whether or not the students were actually learning anything.

She looked at the agenda that she had picked up when she came in. There was nothing on it at all about educational programs.

Mortensen put another flourishing checkmark on his own copy, and moved on to the next topic.

"Right, comments or questions from the public?"

Beth raised her hand.

"Go ahead Mrs. Southwick." Mortensen sounded considerably less than thrilled to invite her to speak.

Beth stood again. Each time she did this, she thought, her knees trembled a little less.

"Thank you, Mr. Chairman," she said. "I haven't been to one of these meetings before, but I have to say I've been a bit surprised by the absence of anything to do with the instructional programs on the agenda. Does the district have any benchmarks for performance that the board monitors to see whether we are getting good value for all the money we are spending?"

She remained on her feet.

It would be an understatement to say that her question was received frostily. There was a lot of eye rolling among administrators and teachers.

"Mrs. Southwick, the instructional program of the district is the responsibility of the superintendent not the board," explained Mortensen.

"So, does that mean that the board is satisfied with the outcomes the superintendent is creating?" asked Beth.

Mortensen looked around at his fellow members, but seeing nobody on the board rushing to answer, he realized he would have to tackle it himself.

"Speaking as one board member, yes," he said and looked down at his agenda, desperately trying to find the next item to move on to.

"Well, in that case, why do you send your own daughter to a private school?"

Beth could hardly believe what had just come out of her mouth. But, all of a sudden she was mad, fighting mad. Her family paid their taxes in order to obtain an education for the children of the community. But everywhere she looked, anyone working to provide that education seemed to have far more concerns about protecting their own turf than in making sure that the students were prepared to go out into the world and be independent. Frankly, it was disgusting.

Mortensen flushed. People in this town didn't talk to him like that. Even if, as someone who had vigorously opposed school choice for others while sending his own children to a private school, he had exposed himself as an abject hypocrite.

"I'm a successful businessman, I can afford it," he stammered.

"Mr. Mortensen, I'm not criticizing you for sending your kids to a great school, quite the contrary in fact. What I find hard to swallow is that you oppose other people, who can't afford to do the same thing, being given the same opportunity. And then you seem to have very little concern about what happens to the kids in the schools that you oversee."

Mortensen appeared ready to explode. He whacked his gavel on the table.

Out of the corner of her eye Beth could see Bob Finn smiling at her.

"We're moving on," Mortensen pronounced. "I didn't come here to be insulted."

The reporter was scribbling frantically.

The meeting lasted another fifteen minutes. As Beth got up to leave she felt a dozen pairs of eyes gazing at her with ill-concealed hatred. She moved out of the door and heard muttering in the room behind her.

Bob Finn followed her out into the parking lot.

"Excuse me," he said, offering a handshake. "We haven't met, but that was really great. I haven't seen Mortensen that flustered in years. They need someone to go in and rattle their cage now and again. Usually nobody will stand up to them"

"Thanks," said Beth. "I'm not sure, though, that I'm really cut out for this confrontational stuff. I'm still shaking like a leaf."

"Oh, that wears off after you do it enough times," Finn replied. "The important thing is not to give up. It may seem as if you didn't achieve anything in there apart from antagonizing them. But the thing is, in this business you never get the dramatic victory. They're not going to admit you're right and make an about turn on policy."

"It's more of a drip feed," he went on. "Every time you speak out in public, or write an article in the paper, you move the process a tiny bit. They wouldn't say anything in there, but they'll be asking questions over the next week or two so that they're prepared next time. Hamlin will catch some stick for allowing them to be exposed like that. He'll be petrified about losing his overpaid sinecure of a job, so he'll say something to his principals about jacking the expectations a bit."

"So who is it that actually is able to create change," asked Beth exasperated. "I've been in a classroom, and the teacher doesn't want to do anything. I've been to parent's evenings and the principal doesn't want to do anything. And now I've been to the board and they don't care either. Who's prepared to stand up and lead the charge?"

"I know. It's a problem isn't it?" admitted Finn. "Maybe you should talk to some folks in the state legislature."

CHAPTER 13

"Once upon a time, America sheltered an Einstein, went to the moon, and gave the world the laser, the electronic computer, nylons, television, and the cure for polio. Today, we are in the process, albeit unwittingly, of abandoning this leadership role."
Leon M. Lederman, Nobel Prize winner in Physics

NOVEMBER 2008

SUNBURY, NEW HAMPSHIRE

It had been a tough road trip and Douglas Southwick was enjoying the relaxation of a cocktail party at Chloe Roberts place.

His trip had taken him to Shanghai for the first time, to visit a vendor's plant. What he had seen had, frankly, stunned him.

Prevailing opinion in the United States was that China was still populated by a billion or more automatons who got out of bed each day for the sole purpose of doing the bidding of the government and the Communist party. Such a structure, Americans told themselves, could never mount a serious economic challenge to the free-wheeling self determination of the Western democracies.

Douglas was under no illusion that China was a free country. Hidden away, but in existence nevertheless, he knew that were still plenty of prisons full of folks whose only crime was possession of sufficient courage and character to question the government's authority.

In contrast, though, what was visible in the streets and businesses of the city was pure, unbridled capitalism, the likes of which he had never seen before.

Outside of his hotel room window, in the couple of hundred yards that he could see before everything faded into the perpetual downtown smog that blanketed the streets, there was the unmistakable bustle of active commerce. Young people thronged the sidewalks, cell phones glued to their ears. Traffic snarled the streets around the clock, with taxi drivers screeching across several lanes, oblivious to the ever present cyclists, to reach the prospect of a lucrative fare promised by an outstretched hand.

There was no sign of workers dressed in Mao suits, of soldiers on the streets, of patriotic songs on the TV or any type of political cult of personality.

He had read somewhere that a quarter of the world's construction cranes were employed in Shanghai. Looking out the window of the taxi that took them from the hotel to the plant, that seemed entirely possible. Development, both upward and outward was demonstrably occurring at a colossal rate. He doubted, somehow, that there were many regulatory obstacles being put in the way of developers who were intent on adding to the city's ever expanding skyline.

In the evenings, as he toured the sprawling downtown area, he passed billboards and storefronts that testified to both the consumer appetite, and the retail availability, for luxury Western brand name goods. Elegant department stores co-existed comfortably with traditional street markets selling counterfeit brands of everything from Rolex watches to North Face parkas. Knock-off DVD's of the latest Hollywood movies were being openly hawked on the street for about a dollar, payable in the currency of your choice to the enterprising young man who had taken his video camera into the local movie theater the night before. Nobody seemed bothered about impediments like intellectual property rights, which might unnecessarily disrupt the flow of otherwise free trade.

Technology was in use everywhere. One night, Douglas' hosts from the plant took him for dinner in the beer garden of an Irish pub. A large crowd of English and Irish ex-patriates had gathered to watch a European soccer game, beamed in by satellite to a gigantic flat panel TV. Douglas had asked a couple of them about life in China.

"It's great mate. Everyone's out to make a buck."

Indeed, as far as business was concerned, there didn't seem to be many other rules. Nothing like OSHA, or environmental concerns, and nobody seemed to have even heard of health insurance.

Douglas got a powerful sense that it would not be long before the tidal wave of entrepreneurial progress would sweep away what remained of government oppression. He felt that, despite an American fixation on the buildup of the Chinese military, there probably wasn't a lot to fear in that regard. After all, why would they want to go and bomb their biggest customer? What concerned him, as an accountant, was their cost base. They enjoyed such a huge price advantage over the West. Combining that with the sort of free enterprise and embrace of technology that he was witnessing with his own eyes, it was hard to see how anything would eventually be manufactured in the developed world.

And where would that leave America and his kids? The more he looked, the more he thought that the only possible salvation would be if his country became one gigantic Silicon Valley. Only innovation would have the value attached to it that could possibly support the American lifestyle. Anybody could manufacture now. The value premium which had been attached to American efficiency at screwing things together on production lines, and which had been responsible for building the world's most powerful nation in the twentieth century, was gone forever.

Nor was there much evidence of any sort of social malaise. The Chinese, at least in the cities, were clearly on a major upward trajectory in terms of lifestyle, but they were far from fat and happy.

"They're working their asses off," Douglas thought.

He noted the emphasis that was placed on education. Parents in Shanghai had more effective school choices than he had himself. Several executives at the plant had their children in private schools, at fees that sounded a lot more reasonable, relative to their incomes, than he could find in New Hampshire.

A lot of the curriculum was geared towards a very high stakes national exit exam. All of the children, from kindergarten onwards, were being taught English.

"That'll come in handy for when they take us over!"

He had sat on the plane on the way home lost in thought. What did it all mean? On the one hand, it seemed hopeful that such a vast nation was seemingly committed to two of history's most effective predictors of an open and peace seeking society: free enterprise and a widespread capability in the English language. But on the other hand the sheer determination to succeed on a massive scale was unmistakably a colossal economic threat to the United States. He had seen nothing like that level of intensity at home. He imagined that is how the energy must have been in America at the dawn of the twentieth century.

Had he looked down as he crossed the California coast he might have seen some of the thousands of empty shipping containers clogging up the port areas. Silent testament to the fact that there was nothing in the United States that Asia wanted Americans to put in them and ship over on the return voyage. These days the things were built with hinges so that they could be folded up and sent back empty without taking up as much space.

Back at home, in Sunbury, the cocktail party at the Roberts' house wound on into the night. Douglas, obsessed now with what he had seen in China, related his stories and concerns to whoever would listen. Even he could tell that he was boring his fellow guests. Nobody really wanted to hear dismal prognosticating. Eventually Beth kicked him on the ankle and he shut up.

Thus silenced by a higher power, Douglas turned his attention to the rest of the room. He noticed Ying Chang, who Beth had introduced to him, in a small adjacent group.

The conversation in his own group droned on. A lot of the guests were parents of school age children. They all wanted to talk about how brilliantly their offspring were doing both athletically and academically. While managing to nod at the appropriate moments, but only feigning interest, he eavesdropped on Ying's circle of friends.

He noticed several accents. The group was made up entirely, he realized, of expatriates.

The talk was of the good life in America. They were all enjoying the airplanes and the swimming pools, the big houses and the disposable income. Travel opportunities that had not been available to them in their countries of origin, because of financial considerations, were now regular events in their lives. They spoke enthusiastically of trips to the West, and to the Caribbean.

Douglas felt a certain pride that all these folks had come to live in his country and were so obviously feeling good about it.

Then Ying said, "Yes, but what about the schools?"

Despite himself, Douglas turned to look at the group.

Silence had fallen. Several folks were staring into their glasses, looking for conversational inspiration.

"Well, is total disaster, no?" said one, in a heavy Eastern European accent.

"Sure, but what you gonna do," replied another. "Go home?"

Silence again.

Douglas noticed that Beth too had turned towards the group. She had been listening as well. He forced himself to face away, but his attention lingered on what they had to say.

It was apparent from the conversation that not one of the eight people making up the group of expatriates thought much of the Sunbury school system, or indeed the American system in general. It occurred to Douglas that they each were tortured by the fact that they were making a deal with the devil. In order to preserve the standard of living that they enjoyed, they were placing their children in schools that lessened their educational attainments relative to what they might have achieved in their country of origin.

Douglas had never really seen immigration to the United States in that light. It was uncomfortable.

CHAPTER 14
"Keep your friends close, and your enemies closer."
Sun-Tzu, Chinese general & military strategist (400 BC)

OCTOBER 2008

SUNBURY, NEW HAMPSHIRE

The day after the school board meeting Jim Mortensen had called several of his friends who had businesses in the area and just happened to be frequent recipients of school and town local government contracts orchestrated by him.

Mortensen had suggested they might want to hint to the editor of the local newspaper that they wouldn't really want any of their advertising appearing anywhere near articles that appeared favorable to criticism of the school district. Might not even want them in the same edition, come to think of it. The editor got the message loud and clear.

Beth had opened the newspaper at breakfast a couple of days later to find her name vilified in the press for the first time.

"Mrs. Southwick should recognize that the education of our children needs to be left up to the professionals," bellowed a certain Joan Simons, who apparently was the president of the local teachers' union.

"Very divisive comments. Not helpful at all," was how Mortensen had labeled her observations.

"We welcome constructive criticism," Superintendent Hamlin had claimed. Beth thought that was a bit of a stretch. "But we would hope that it would always stop short of this type of bashing of people who work very hard on behalf of the community's youngsters."

The paper had not even invited comment from Beth.

At first, a chill had gone through her whole body. It was not pleasant to be labeled a pariah in your own community. She could just picture Pam Jackson's satisfaction.

"My God," she thought, I just asked a couple of questions. "It's my kid, for heaven's sake. They make it sound like they own him!"

Bob Finn had called her.

"Hope you don't mind me calling you out of the blue like this," he said. "I got your number out of the book. Just thought you might need a bit of a morale boost after what those swine said in the paper. You should be proud of yourself. They only say stuff like that when they're worried that you might have had an impact."

He told her that there would probably be a phone call. And what its purpose would be.

"The next thing they'll try to do is to buy you off," he told her. "No, not with money. They'll offer you some position in their little political machine. A committee post or something, where they can keep an eye on you."

"And that's supposed to make me happy?" Beth asked.

"Remember, " Finn told her. "Most of the folks they recruit don't have a lot going for them. Even some minor committee spot makes them feel important. Gives them a taste of power. Often that's enough."

"And if I turn it down?"

"Well then," Finn chuckled "It'll be war, won't it?"

When the call came, it was not from Mortensen.

"Mrs. Southwick?" the caller said. "Hi, my name's Ron Courmeyer. Do you have a minute to chat?"

"Sure, what about?" Beth thought she recognized the name from one of the citizens' access TV channel shows she caught now and again. She had a vague image of a rather self assured individual who hosted chat shows on local issues, but only ever invited people who agreed with him as guests.

"We haven't met," Courmeyer began. "But I work with other volunteers in town on a lot of the boards and committees that keep things running smoothly around here."

"Oh, you mean with folks like Jim Mortensen?"

"Yes, that's right. Jim's a good friend of mine. Great guy. Make's a huge effort for this community. He was 'Citizen of the Year' a couple of years ago, you know."

"You don't say?" Beth allowed a hint of sarcasm in her voice. "I didn't exactly feel the brotherly love oozing out of the things he said about me in the newspaper the other day. 'Divisive' was the term he used, I think."

Courmeyer laughed.

"Oh, don't worry about that, Beth. These newspaper guys make up all sorts of stuff. Is it all right if I call you Beth?"

"Actually, no, it isn't."

There was a pause on the other end of the line. That answer wasn't in the script apparently. Beth had a pleasing mental picture of Courmeyer frantically flipping through pages to see if he could find how Jim Mortensen advised him to answer that response.

"Oh! Err, okay then, Mrs. Southwick, well, anyway, the reason for my call is that a lot of us who work in the community interest have taken note of what you've been saying. We think yours is a voice that should be heard in town, and we think there's a better way of achieving that. We want to help you."

"In what way would that be?"

"Well, with respect, Mrs. Southwick, we have a saying around here. 'We can disagree without being disagreeable'."

Beth rolled her eyes. Courmeyer had recited the hackneyed phrase as if he had been the one that coined it. Beth had heard it used so many times before, always when one side of an argument wanted to attempt to silence the other by publicly characterizing them as 'disagreeable'.

"So, you think I'm being disagreeable because I want my children to learn proper Math?"

"No, no, that's not it at all," Courmeyer had adopted a patronizing tone that set Beth's teeth on edge. Had he been in the room she would have thrown something at him. "It's just that we've found that there are ways to get your point across without unnecessarily antagonizing folks."

"Right," said Beth, thinking that she had seen the results of that philosophy in the instruction delivered in Mike's classroom. "Mr. Courmeyer, what do you have in mind?"

"Well, it just so happens that a vacancy has come up on the school district's curriculum committee. We all just thought it would be great if you could direct some of your obvious passion for education into a productive slot like that. If you wanted to do it, we could probably get you appointed really quickly."

"I'll bet you could," thought Beth.

"Mr. Courmeyer," she asked. "What's the makeup of that committee?"

"Oh, there's about twenty folks on it. About half of them are teachers, and the other half are mainly parents. I know a bunch of them."

"I see. And they were presumably the one's responsible for recommending the 'Learning Through Discovery' system for the elementaries?"

"Yeah, that's right," Courmeyer gushed. "What a huge advance that's been. I remember sitting in on a presentation they gave before we adopted that program. They were all really excited by the potential for what it could do for the kids."

"So it was pretty much unanimous?" Beth asked, wondering if Courmeyer had actually been briefed on anything she had been saying for the past few weeks.

"Oh, yes Ma'am, I believe it was."

"They must think I'm a complete idiot," Beth thought to herself. "They want to bury me out of sight of the TV cameras and the reporters, battling against a permanent twenty to one majority until I get bored and give up."

Beth tried to make her voice as patronizing as Courmeyer's had been.

"Well, Mr. Courmeyer, I think I might just have to pass on that one, but it was so nice of you to think of me."

Even down a phone line, Beth could sense a stiffening. There was another pause.

"You know what, Beth, this is the best offer you're going to get. If I were you, I'd take it. Folks have tried to get their way in this town before. It hasn't always turned out that well."

Beth just laughed.

"Let me guess. You got that line from a Clint Eastwood movie, right? Thanks for calling, Mr. Courmeyer, but I really do have to go now."

She hung up the phone.

CHAPTER 15

"Politics is supposed to be the second oldest profession. I have come to realize that it bears a very close resemblance to the first."
Ronald Reagan, President of the United States

NOVEMBER 2008

CONCORD, NEW HAMPSHIRE

Driving from Sunbury to Concord, Beth mulled over how her outlook, indeed in some ways her life, had changed in just a few short weeks.

That she had become obsessed with public policy she wouldn't deny. Douglas thought it was all getting a bit too much.

But there was a thrill at being involved in the process that she hadn't experienced before. She woke up every morning thinking about schools and what she might do next. It was energizing.

It wasn't, however, all fun and games. The article in the local newspaper, about what she and Bob Finn had said at the board meeting, had initially made her feel sick to her stomach.

After a while, some of the chill was replaced by anger and a fierce determination.

In the following days she had noticed that the act of getting on her feet and speaking out had changed the way she was perceived in the community. The reaction among her friends was mixed. Several clearly thought it was now dangerous to be associated with her. Folks who would have previously been quite happy to get together for coffee now, all of a sudden, had all sorts of other pressing engagements they had to attend to instead. It was as if they thought that the "Friends of Beth Southwick" group might be socially ostracized in Sunbury.

Others, the ones with a bit more character and backbone as far as Beth was concerned, were happy to remain as friends and supporters, but there were still limits.

Chloe Roberts had called her.

"Quite the celebrity around town these days," she said.

"Or the villain of the piece, more like," Beth replied.

Chloe said she had watched it all on TV.

"I thought old Jim was going to come across the desk at you when you said that about his daughter being in private school," she laughed. "Why don't you write a response in the paper? An editorial or letter to the editor."

"I hadn't thought of that, but I might, would you like to co-author it with me?"

There was a pause on the other end of the line.

"Let me think about it," Chloe had said, suddenly hesitant. "My husband has a business here in town. We have to be very careful. It's easy to get a lot of customers all ticked off."

After they had hung up the phones. Beth had been struck by the fact that the reach of the school district was almost sinister. They decided what was right and wrong for your kids to learn, how much it would cost, and then intimidated anyone who might raise a voice in objection.

"Like Big Brother and 1984," she thought.

But the fear factor was not only in one direction. She recalled seeing Alice Farmington in the supermarket the previous day. Alice, who was so tough when surrounded by her friends and allies in the board room, had pretended not to see Beth and dived into the frozen food aisle to avoid a confrontation. But Beth had caught the fleeting look of recognition and panic on Alice's face, and had felt a surge of confidence.

She remembered once hearing one of Winston Churchill's speeches, eviscerating Mussolini and his gang.

"They're afraid of *words*," the great man had sneered, with a degree of condescension that only he could muster.

It was starting to seem to Beth that, in politics, it didn't matter whether you were talking great affairs of state, or control over a few thousand kids in local schools. Everywhere you went there were little tin pot dictators hell bent on protecting their turf by stifling dissent.

Still looking for someone, or some entity, that would place the interests of students and families ahead of the interests of the politicians and institutions, she had taken Bob Finn's advice and put in a couple of calls to her district's members of the New Hampshire House of Representatives.

The New Hampshire House prided itself on being the third largest deliberative legislative body in the English speaking world. With over four hundred members, it was surpassed only by the United States House and the British parliament.

Another quirk was that members were only paid two hundred dollars per year for their services. On the one hand, it meant that the body was truly a citizen legislature, nobody was going to get rich being a "state rep". But on the other hand, the lack of a meaningful salary meant that the House was populated by a mixture of a few wealthy folks who could afford to work for nothing or had a spouse who brought home the bacon, and a large number of retirees living off their pensions.

Beth hadn't known any of the six representatives for Sunbury. But she had found their names and phone numbers on the state Web site and arranged a couple of meetings.

Bill Holmes was a Democrat whose assignments included the House Education Committee. Her first appointment was with him.

Holmes was in his fourth term. Like many other members he was a retired teacher who had worked his entire career in the New Hampshire public school system.

Historically, New Hampshire had been considered a rock solid Republican state, and it came as a great surprise to Holmes when the Democrats assumed a majority in the House in 2006. Although he did not aspire to any sort of leadership role, all of a sudden his vote now almost always appeared on the majority side and he derived considerable satisfaction from the fact that he was making laws.

Although he had not taught in a number of years, he still wore the little "Hands around the World" lapel pin, depicting a diverse group of children holding hands, that signified his ongoing commitment to the profession and its practitioners. Or at least to the ones who earned their daily bread in the public, not private, system.

He lived comfortably, but not luxuriously, and one of his objectives in the legislature, and on his committee, was to see that teachers who followed him were provided with the respect, working conditions and incomes that he felt had been denied to him during his career. The teachers' union annual rankings of representatives always placed him in the top decile of all representatives based on their voting records. He was proud of that although, in truth, he never even read a lot of the bills on which he was asked to make a decision. He just went along with whatever the party leadership asked him to do.

Representatives, unless members of the party leadership, did not have their own offices. So Beth and Holmes had arranged to meet in the lobby of the capitol building.

It was not very often at all that any of his constituents came to visit him, and Beth hadn't mentioned her purpose. So Holmes was quite happy to leave his committee for an hour, which was indescribably boring work anyway, to see what it was that she had in mind. He anticipated that she would think he was someone important, and he always liked that.

It was a kindly looking man, Beth thought, with a thatch of silver hair and a slightly stooped gait who approached her.

"Mrs. Southwick?" he inquired.

Beth nodded.

"How nice of you to come. I'm Bill Holmes," he smiled. "May I suggest we go downstairs where we can chat?"

They each selected a pastry and a cup of coffee and took a seat in the cozy little cafeteria in the basement of the building.

"So, what's on your mind, and how can I help," asked Holmes.

Later, with a bit more experience in how the battle lines of education politics were drawn, Beth would chuckle at the fact that she had not looked up Holmes' bio on the state web-site. Had she known his background she wouldn't have wasted her time.

While Holmes listened attentively, she talked for several minutes about her experiences with the local schools, and her fears for what it all meant for the future economically, for both her own children and the country as a whole.

"Oh, Lord," thought Holmes. "Just another public school basher."

" I looked up a couple of things on the internet," she was reaching into her bag. "I found the results for the Advanced Placement Exams for New Hampshire. Did you know that only about one out of every twenty-five students in the public system passes the AP Calculus exam? And hardly any pass a foreign language. And we're spending thirteen thousand dollars per year per student now."

Holmes glanced at the page, but made no effort to take in the details. He laughed politely.

"Well, that's college level material," he said. "And besides, it would be very dangerous to base our education system on teaching to a test."

"Why?" asked Beth. "I mean, what is there in the AP Calculus exam that is not a good thing for any student to know. Especially now that they're heading into such a technological world."

"Oh, I don't know. I never was much for Math," admitted Holmes.

"There you go again," thought Beth. Whenever the results are bad, they discredit the test, or even the whole concept of testing.

"Anyway, what I wanted to talk to you about was the fact that if you look closer you find that students in private schools pass these exams at about four times the rate of public school students. Don't you find that worrying?"

"Not particularly, actually," the kindly look on Holmes' face had slipped a little, Beth noted.

"But, if the private schools work so much better, wouldn't it seem to make sense to use them to provide publicly funded education?" asked Beth.

Holmes sighed.

"Mrs. Southwick, if you've come here to try to persuade me to support vouchers, I'm afraid you're talking to the wrong representative. The public schools are one of the fundamental underpinnings of our society, and I, for one, will never vote to drain desperately needed funds away from them to private schools."

'Draining', Beth knew, was the favorite financial argument of the public school monopoly lobby. Their ploy was to insist that all of the costs of running a school were fixed, so that if one child were removed, along with his share of the funding, then there would be insufficient funds to pay the electricity bill, or the superintendent's salary, neither of which would change as a result of the subtraction of one or more students.

Beth could actually see some logic to the argument, but Douglas had pointed out the flaws.

"Well, they might have a case if the system were not expanding," he explained. "But, given that we're spending millions on new public facilities, you could equally well make the argument that those are 'draining' from the ones that are already there! Their argument is nonsense. What they call 'draining' is a function of expansion. From a financial viewpoint, it doesn't matter who owns or runs the building."

So Beth was well prepared.

"Let me ask you a question," she said. "You're supporting the new elementary school that the board wants in Sunbury, right?" She knew the answer already. Holmes had a written a letter to the editor in the local paper explaining what a vital 'investment' it was.

"Of course," Holmes agreed

"Well, let me ask you this. Suppose the law did allow vouchers. And suppose the school that was being proposed was going to service exactly the same kids, at exactly the same cost, but was going to be a private institution, with fees paid by vouchers. Would that be 'draining', and would you support that school as an investment?"

Holmes looked puzzled for a moment. He'd never heard anyone explain away his precious draining argument like that.

'I don't support vouchers under any circumstances," he stammered out.

"Let me get this straight, Representative. Even if it wasn't going to cost more money, and if, statistically, it had a chance of producing significantly better academic results, you would oppose it for our community if it wasn't staffed by the teachers' union? Even though you think a new school is needed?"

Beth noted a bead of sweat on Holmes' brow. This meeting wasn't going as he had planned at all.

"Well, it's a hypothetical question," he objected. "Besides vouchers are completely unconstitutional."

"Well, the Supreme Court of the United States doesn't seem to think so. Have you ever read the *Zelman* decision?" Beth retorted, enjoying the fact that she obviously knew far more about the subject than Holmes.

"The what decision?" asked Holmes.

"*Zelman vs Simmons Harris*," Beth repeated. In a sudden burst of clarity, she understood that it didn't matter what logic was presented to Representative Holmes, he was going to vote to continue the monopoly of his pals in the union, and they were going to continue to work to re-elect him. Student achievement was simply not on his radar. He was working for the other side.

She couldn't see a lot of point in confrontation, so she made small talk while they finished their coffee.

"Are you going to spend the day here," Holmes inquired.

"Well, I'll be here for a while anyway. I have another meeting arranged."

"You might want to spend some time in the public gallery of the House, if you haven't been here before," suggested Holmes. "There is a session this afternoon."

"Oh, really. What's being debated?"

"I'm not sure of all the bills, honestly, but I do know that there's been quite a lot of talk about changing the official state bird."

Beth worked hard to suppress the primal scream that was rising in her throat. The economy was going to Hell in a hand basket, the kids couldn't perform basic math, and her elected representatives were spending their days elevating the status of blue tits. She smiled politely, thanked Holmes for meeting with her and headed off for her other appointment.

She had arranged to meet Representative David Matheson, Republican, outside his committee room. They shook hands and he gestured towards a bench in the hallway where they could sit.

Beth told her story again. She ended by describing her frustration with her previous meeting. Matheson didn't interrupt.

"Yes, it's a huge problem isn't it?" he agreed. "I wish I could be more encouraging, but as you're obviously learning, the union, the administrators and the school boards have a huge influence here."

Beth pulled out her papers with the AP results. Matheson pored over them for several minutes, asking a question now and then.

"Look," Beth said, pointing at the bottom line. "Altogether in the New Hampshire public system we got about four thousand AP passes in all subjects combined. And, according to the Department of Education website, we're spending two and a half billion dollars on primary and secondary education. So that means it costs six hundred thousand dollars for every AP pass!"

"I didn't realize it was quite that bad," he said finally. "That's pretty scary, isn't it?"

"What can we do?" asked Beth.

"To be completely honest with you, very little at this point," Matheson answered. "The last serious attempt at vouchers was in 2004, when there were Republican majorities in the House and Senate and a Republican governor. Vouchers were also a plank in the Republican party platform. You would have thought that we could've got something through then. House Bill 1353, I think it was. If I remember rightly seventy Republicans voted against it in the House and it failed by a single vote."

"Why on Earth would they vote against their party platform?" asked Beth.

"Fear," explained Matheson. "Look around you. This place is like an old folks' home. They all come here to socialize, and the title of Representative makes them feel important. They're all petrified that they might get voted out at the next election and the best way to ensure that doesn't happen is to avoid doing anything that will rile up the other party. The teachers are incredibly organized. The night before an important education vote, every representative gets dozens of phone calls telling him that if he doesn't vote the way the union wants, they'll target him at the next election."

"So they just cave?"

"That's about right," Matheson confirmed.

Beth skipped the debate about designating a new state bird.

Sitting at her computer that night she looked up the legislation that David Matheson had told her about, House Bill 1353, in 2004. The votes of each representative were recorded in the legislative section of the state web site. She scanned down the list. Yea, Nay, Yea, Nay, Nay. Halfway down she stopped, stunned. David Matheson, it read, "Nay".

"Et tu, Brute," she thought.

PART 2

THE ALTERNATIVE

CHAPTER 16

"You do not become a dissident just because you decide one day to take up this most unusual career. You are thrown into it by your personal sense of responsibility, combined with a complex set of external circumstances. You are cast out of the existing structures and placed in a position of conflict with them. It begins as an attempt to do your work well, and ends with being branded an enemy of society."
Vaclav Havel, President of the Czech Republic and former dissident

NOVEMBER 2008

SUNBURY, NEW HAMPSHIRE

Beth Southwick's introduction to school politics over the previous few months had led her to some fundamental conclusions, as well as some sobering realizations.

It was clear to her that the type of haphazard hit-and-run raids that she had made so far on the public school citadel, even though they may have created some temporary headaches for the officials, were not sufficiently organized to make a substantive difference to her children's classroom experience. To have a really effective impact, she knew that she needed a comprehensive strategy and a campaign that would hit with far more force than she had been able to muster thus far. She spent a great deal of time contemplating the structure that such an effort would have to take.

She was not sufficiently naïve to believe that success was guaranteed, or that she could become some sort of educational Joan of Arc riding to the rescue of a nation. In fact, she thought it highly unlikely that she could score anything resembling a political knock-out. But, every time that she felt like giving up, the fear that her children would be left bereft of the skills that they would one day need to thrive in a much more competitive world rekindled her determination.

Beth felt that she now had a good grasp on the personal and political motivations of all the parties involved in public education. The completed picture was not an attractive one. In fact, it was a depressing and uninterrupted continuum of greed, power grabs and self interest as far as the eye could see.

She understood fully now why Chloe had told her that the institution of public education was often referred to as "The Blob". The whole thing was like a thousand pound wrestler who defeated opponents effortlessly simply by sitting on them until all resistance vanished.

What was remarkable about "The Blob", and possibly indicated by the gelatinous nature of its moniker, was that it never fractured. Absolute power in political organizations, Beth knew, often ended when splinter groups within the organization began to covet authority.

Nothing like that seemed to occur in public education. Instead, everyone involved, from the school board, to the administration, to the teachers, and even a lot of the parents, marched in lockstep to the beat of a single drum sounding out its endlessly uniform rhythm of self-esteem.

It obviously didn't matter to the Mortensens or the Courmeyers, or the Superintendent Hamlins, or the Joan Simons that their unwillingness to allow anyone to escape from the clutches of public school orthodoxy might well result in the whole country going off the economic cliff. They, and, Beth was sure, thousands just like them across the country, were the pied pipers of mediocrity. Millions followed, blind and unquestioning, in their wake. All was well with them, just as long as the parade continued, and they, the chosen few, remained firmly in the vanguard.

After her visit to Concord, she could confidently add state politicians to her list of "no-shows" on educational standards. Furthermore, she had no indication that anyone in Washington DC was prepared to take a stand. The Democratic party was totally in the pockets of the unions, The Republican party had school choice in their platform, but all it generated was a lot of huffing and puffing. The fact was that her cause was generational, and, in a world of political quick fixes, long term benefits were not on the radar screen of elected officials. Changing standards in schools, however desperately important to the futures of students in elementary schools today, would not show a significant benefit to the country as a whole for twenty years after enactment. Until then, it was a politician's nightmare. Lots of hard work for your constituents, regular beatings for yourself from the all powerful educational lobby and no immediate visible return. Hardly a recipe for re-election. To stay in office, in the 21st century, a much better strategy was to focus on providing government handouts, and avoid education like the plague.

Implementation of a widespread voucher program, Beth now knew, required a perfect alignment of all the political stars. The governor's office, and both houses of the legislature needed to be populated by folks with a very different set of priorities than the people she had just encountered in Concord.

Even if the legislative branch could be persuaded to enact school choice laws, there would be years of constitutional challenges before anything actually happened. The Supreme Court of New Hampshire would almost certainly seek cover behind the state's dismal and xenophobic Blaine amendment. That meant that the United States Supreme Court would effectively have to outlaw the Blaines nationwide before full school choice could prevail in New Hampshire.

The disappointing reality was that in a Blaine amendment state like New Hampshire, there was a higher probability of paying for private school fees by winning the lottery than that all of those outcomes were going to combine in her favor within the next few years. The power and inflexibility of "The Blob" would ensure that school choice vouchers, however worthy of her intense and prolonged efforts, were not going to happen in time to let her own children escape the mind-numbing clutches of the public school monopoly.

When she had first heard about vouchers, and the solid financial arguments in support of their usage, it had seemed such a sensible concept that she had initially assumed that it could not be that difficult to make everyone else feel the same way. Who wouldn't be for more choice and lower costs, after all? But that was before she learned that it was the providers of public education, not the consumers, who were calling the shots.

She saw that she had prematurely set her heart on the possibility of being able to send her children to a school that was much more closely aligned with her own ideas about education. It was a crushing blow to her to have to recognize that political considerations, not educational ones, would deny her the choice that she craved.

But it was what it was. If vouchers, however financially sensible and however advantageous as a method of engineering real reform, were off the table as a realistic goal for her efforts to change her children's educational experience, then she would reluctantly have to discard that approach and seek other avenues.

She took stock of her prospects. The situation in regard to advocating reform of the existing system, however challenging, was not without hope. There were some undeniable weaknesses in the system's defenses. Her thoughts turned to how she could exploit those areas.

First and foremost, the academic results that the monopoly was able to produce were truly awful. Despite the propaganda spewed forth by public school supporters, there was no doubt that a substantial part of the community was heartily disappointed by objective measures of what the students were achieving. The school district routinely buried, distorted or denied the importance of test scores. Beth guessed that if she were to publicize academic results at every opportunity, she could probably shine a much more revealing spotlight on curriculum and instructional issues. That should draw in some supporters on her side. Two could play the propaganda game.

Secondly, the dead hand of uniformity was hard at work producing the lousy test scores. The district served several thousand families, and, if asked, each might produce a different definition of what constituted "a good education". The administration and the board, however, were intent on finding and delivering a single uniform solution that they would then label "best practice" and expect all participants to rally behind. That uniform solution, in order to cater to the entire community, had of necessity to set a very low hurdle. An army marches at the pace of the slowest.

Beth sensed a fundamental discrepancy there between the approach of the institution and the bedrock values of its customers. Perhaps that was a seam that she could rip apart. Americans generally have an aversion to monopolies and standardization. They want choices in regard to decisions that impact them directly, particularly when those decisions pertain to children that they consider exceptional.

Chloe had told her, at the outset, how much the school districts dreaded variance in educational outcomes.

"If none of the kids can do math, hardly anybody is unhappy," Chloe had said. "But if, all of a sudden, your neighbor's kid can do Calculus and speak a foreign language, and your kid can't, that's when you start asking questions. A lot of it comes down to jealousy in the end."

Uniformity was the keystone of "Blob" philosophy. School district officials successfully promoted the politically correct concept that if one child learned more than another then something unfair must have happened.

Beth, on the other hand, believed that equal opportunity was represented by allowing every child to go just as far and as fast as their motivation and capabilities could take them. If the result was wildly different outcomes, then so be it.

She recognized, in her approach, the old political argument of collectivism versus individuality, repackaged in the setting of classrooms. Sunbury was a conservative town. She was going to bet that there were a lot of people who thought as she did.

The last thing she wanted to do, however, was to try to force her opinion on anyone who didn't share it. She knew, from having the school district compel an approach that she did not support on her children, what an uncomfortable situation that was. Instead, her suggestion would be, given that there was quite obviously a plethora of different views, maybe the students needed to be grouped differently. In the elementaries, for example, there could be some of the 'Learning Through Discovery' classrooms where students would spend time coloring and singing songs, if that's what their parents wanted. Other students, in separate classrooms, would devote far more time to the three R's in preparation for the exacting classes that would lead to AP exams later in their school careers.

The Blob's argument against vouchers was always that it would "drain" funds away from them. They successfully, if inaccurately, demonized as a thief anyone who proposed purchasing educational services elsewhere. But, if she presented her suggestion as creating an alternative that neither established a new administrative framework, nor diverted any funds, it would be much harder for supporters of the status quo to find grounds for attack.

She guessed that, over time, all the available metrics such as state assessment tests, SAT scores, and AP passes would tilt heavily in favor of those who selected the more traditional environment.

Especially, in a wealthy community like Sunbury, when it came to college admissions that were inextricably linked with parental social status, even parents who currently advocated most vociferously against raising expectations on students would not want their own children following a pedagogical approach that was demonstrably and measurably disadvantageous.

"Jealousy," Chloe had said. So, jealousy it would be. That was how she would build her campaign. If the district could appeal to parents by the politics of equality, deflecting dissent by an egalitarian herd mentality and safety in numbers, then she would offer a different vision. One that would encompass choice at no cost within the public school setting. A choice that would not be impeded by Blaine amendments or insipid politicians in the State House. A choice that would emphasize measurable individual excellence, and encourage parents to come to their own conclusion that their children had better start running or they would fall behind.

CHAPTER 17

"To avoid criticism, say nothing, do nothing, be nothing."
Albert Einstein, Physicist

NOVEMBER 2008

SCHOOL BOARD MEETING ROOM, SUNBURY, NEW HAMPSHIRE

As she drove towards her second school board meeting, armed this time with prepared comments about her suggestions, conflicting thoughts hammered away in her brain.

The part of her that still shied away from controversy and publicity was silently screaming, "What on earth are you doing?"

But the reality was that despite her recent activism, and despite Bob Finn's comments that she might start to see some changes, there was nothing very different coming home from school in Mike's backpack. An awful lot of classroom time still seemed to be taken up with coloring, and cut and paste.

And so another voice kept creeping into her head.

"They're your kids."

She pulled into the little parking lot outside the school district office. A familiar chill went down her spine. The lot that had been almost empty at the last meeting, was now overflowing to the point that cars were parked on the verges.

She wondered what was on the agenda that could trigger so much interest.

"Just my luck," she thought. "An audience."

She knew that to promote her ideas she had to get out in front of people. But that didn't make it any easier. She had read somewhere that fear of public speaking was one of the world's most pervasive phobias. She seriously considered turning around and going home, but a fleeting mental image of another set of bunny ears and the hot glue gun drove her forward.

As she entered the building into the little lobby area, she could see through the glass panel into the meeting room that there was not going be the sparse attendance that had characterized the previous meeting, and others she had seen on TV.

In fact, the crowd had overflowed into the lobby. As she entered, several faces turned towards her, and the bustle of conversation died down. Someone opened the door for her, and she moved into the meeting room. Once again the sounds of cheery conversation were replaced by an eerie quiet.

There were no seats available, so she picked up the handouts from the little table at the side of the room and stood against the wall. She felt eyes boring into her. The atmosphere told her there was not a lot of need to study the agenda. It might as well have been a menu, with herself listed as the main course.

It was her first taste of a teachers' union flame out. A threat had been perceived. The tom-tom drums had beaten, and the clan had gathered to protect their turf before things got out of hand.

Beth did not know it, but the union maintained highly effective 'phone trees' that they used to communicate information. Whenever a turnout was needed to support a political objective, teacher A called B and C. Then B called D and E and so on. It wasn't a huge effort for anyone to make two phone calls, but the system, combined with the union's enthusiasm for political causes that advanced its objectives and control, was astonishingly effective at rapidly generating a mob whenever one was needed.

Beth looked around the room. There was not a friendly face in sight. No sign of Bob Finn or Chloe Roberts. Her stomach was turning somersaults. She knew how the Christians must have felt in the Roman Coliseum.

Mortensen sat in his customary spot at the top of the horseshoe table, reading the papers in front of him and pretending that it was quite normal that a crowd had assembled for the meeting. He knew exactly what was about to happen, Joan Simons, the President of the union, had told him that a deputation would be attending. It was even better that Beth Southwick had showed up. She was going to catch it right between the eyes.

"This'll teach that little cow to try to embarrass me in public about my family," he thought, remembering her questions about his personal use of school choice for his daughter.

He allowed the clock to run a minute or two after the official starting time. No point in cutting into the tension that he could feel building in the room. He glanced quickly at Beth, and could tell she was terrified. Despite himself, he felt a momentary admiration that she had the guts to stand there by herself. He guessed that she, too, had figured out why everyone was there.

"OK," he thought. "She's had her chance to leave. Let's light the barbecue."

"I call the meeting to order," he announced.

He moved rapidly through the formalities of minutes and resignations.

On the phone, he had promised Joan Simons that he would not keep her members out too late attending to their human sacrifice.

"Well," he said. "I recognize that we have a number of our valued faculty in the audience tonight. I'm sure we'd all like them to be able to get home early so that they can do their grading and preparation. So I'll just suspend the regular order of the agenda for a few minutes and allow them to say what's on their mind this evening. Do we have a spokesperson?"

Joan Simons stood.

"Yes, Ms. Simons," acknowledged Mortensen.

"Joan Simons, president of The Sunbury Education Association," she identified herself.

Beth recognized the name as being one of the letter writers who had taken her to task in the newspaper.

"Mr. Chairman," Simons went on. "Lately there have been two separate incidents where the integrity and professionalism of the teaching staff in Sunbury has been brought into question. At both a parent meeting and a board meeting, Mrs. Beth Southwick, a parent of a student at Sunbury Elementary, has questioned the teaching methods, the curriculum and the quality of the educational results in our school district."

Several glances were shot in Beth's direction. She remembered the friendly welcome she had been given when she had been cutting up plastic bags in Mike's classroom.

"They all love you as long as you pay your taxes and keep your mouth shut," she thought to herself. The atmosphere was thick with contempt and self righteous indignation. She was trembling slightly.

Simons, emboldened by the attendance of several dozen members of her army, was clearly feeling confident of victory.

"Mr. Chairman, " she went on. "In light of these unwarranted attacks, my members have asked that the board members and the superintendent reaffirm their unequivocal confidence and support for the quality of the teaching that is provided, day in and day out, for the children of the Sunbury community."

There was a murmur of approval from the assembled group, and several more hostile looks towards Beth.

Joan Simons wasn't finished.

"We would also request, Mr. Chairman, that the board emphasizes that policy requires that all questions be brought up first with the classroom teacher, and then privately with the building principal before anything can be addressed at superintendent or board level."

More murmurs of assent. Joan Simons sat down.

Mortensen was absolutely in his element. The TV cameras were rolling, and once he skewered Beth Southwick in public, the union folks who turned out in droves to support him at elections were going to owe him a big favor. It just couldn't be any better.

There was complete silence in the room. Mortensen paused and frowned, milking the situation for all it was worth. All eyes were on him.

"As I think I was quoted in the newspaper last week, I think it is very regrettable that a member of the community should seek to denigrate the efforts of our faculty. I wish it hadn't happened and I quite understand why your membership is so upset.

"Speaking for myself, but I think with the support of all board members and the superintendent, I continue to believe that the education offered in the Sunbury public schools is never anything less than world class and best practice." He paused and looked around at the other members, who all nodded enthusiastically, as did Superintendent Hamlin.

Mortensen looked back at Joan Simons who Beth thought did not yet appear satisfied that her ruffled feathers had been sufficiently soothed.

Alice Farmington obviously picked up on that fact and decided to try to earn herself a few Brownie points while Mortensen seemed to have temporarily shot his bolt.

"I would just like to add, Mr. Chairman, as a parent as well as a board member, that we should remember that Sunbury has frequently been recognized in the past for its outstanding school system. Awards have included 'New Hampshire School System of the Year' in 2005," which, although she didn't mention it, just happened to coincide with Alice's term on the state awards committee.

Mortensen was thinking she had said enough. It was one thing to support him, but he didn't need Alice getting any ideas about currying favor with the union.

But the love fest continued unabated.

"And we mustn't forget either," Alice was unstoppable. "That the High School was categorized as an 'Exemplary Educational Institution' by the Federal Department of Education a few years before that."

The banner commemorating that distinction still hung in the lobby of the High School. Mortensen's memories of the details were as faded as the cloth that made up the flag. But he did recall how he had rigged the lottery that they had held at half time of the basketball game when the judges from the Education Department had attended as part of their evaluation process. They each returned to Washington with a couple of hundred dollars in their pockets, wrote glowing reports about the school's fundraising efforts, and the award arrived about a month later.

Joan Simons appeared mollified at last. She stood.

"Thank you, Mr. Chairman, I shall deliver that message to my members." She looked directly at Beth. "I am sure that they will be happy to know that the vast majority of the community, represented here by the board, are grateful for their efforts and skills."

A smattering of applause rippled around the room. Almost everyone in the audience started to get up to leave.

Beth raised her hand.

"Mr. Chairman, may I say a few words?"

Mortensen was surprised that she hadn't been knocked out of the game by the intimidation factor of being so heavily outnumbered, and by the vehemence of the mood of the teachers present.

Again, he found himself impressed by the intestinal fortitude that he knew it took for her to speak up. His political instinct urged caution. Although he held every card in the situation in front of him, it would be possible for him to overplay his hand and generate a backlash.

"Mrs. Southwick, are you sure? Feelings are running a little high here tonight."

Alice Farmington, looking panicked, interrupted.

"Mr. Chairman, I'm not sure that we need to further antagonize our faculty unnecessarily."

Without looking at Alice, Mortensen held up his hand to her and nodded to Beth that she could continue.

"Thank you, Mr. Chairman."

Several members of the audience sat back down. Others left. Beth waited a moment for the commotion to die down.

"Mr. Chairman, as you know, I am new to the business of local politics," she began. "And I can tell you it has certainly been an eye-opener over the last few weeks. I am a taxpayer, and also, as a parent, a consumer of the services that those taxes support. As such I have a particular interest in precisely what it is that those funds are used to buy. "

The television camera in the corner of the room beamed the scene into homes all around Sunbury.

"Whenever I read articles in the paper about school philosophy, it seems that the theme most emphasized is one of tolerance and inclusion, often at the expense of any focus on pure academics. So, it is amazing to me, frankly, that just the act of my asking a couple of questions at public meetings could trigger such an extraordinary reaction.

"I can't say that, tonight, I feel particularly tolerated or included. In fact, I would have to tell you that 'bullied' is probably the word that best characterizes my emotions at the moment."

The room was completely silent.

Joan Simons was studying the floor carefully. It was just beginning to dawn on her that the evening might not end up going entirely according to plan.

Beth felt that elation, transcending all others, that comes only to the nervous public speaker on the rare occasions when the words tumble out effortlessly, and the audience falls rapt in its attention.

Mortensen, too, felt the momentum swinging away from him.

Beth continued.

"It seems to me that all of the big problems, in any field, occur when one individual, or one group, assumes that it has absolute knowledge, and tries to force an opinion or point of view on everyone else. Now, I don't think it's a secret to anyone, at this point, that I believe in a much more traditional brand of education than is being served up in the classrooms of Sunbury. My personal view is that we should be teaching multiplication tables to whichever first graders can handle that, and asking them to write book reports. There are definitely a number of our students that are capable, and to deny them that opportunity in favor of endless cut and paste activities, seems almost criminally negligent to me."

That brought a groan of disapproval from the audience.

"But I don't want to force that opinion on anyone else, and make that the only option. I just want a choice, that's all. I think a lot of other parents think that too."

From the back of the room someone murmured, "Where are they, then?"

"Probably safe at home, avoiding this lynch mob," Beth thought, but allowed the comment to go unanswered.

She persisted. She had come to the meeting to lay out an alternative scenario, one in which concrete achievement goals were supported by more aggressive instructional practices.

"I've looked at the budget for this year. In this tiny town of Sunbury we're spending sixty-five million dollars each year on the school systems. Shouldn't the policy of this board be to look a little more at the results that we buy for all that spending."

The groan reached a crescendo. More of a collective snort of indignation. She had stuck a knife into the central nervous system of the Sunbury faculty, and all of their colleagues nationwide. She had suggested the unthinkable. That they might be evaluated based on the measurable achievements of their students.

Mortensen sensed his moment to seize back the initiative.

"Mrs. Southwick, we have a very busy agenda tonight. I think this is something you should take up, as Ms. Simons suggested, with the classroom teacher."

Alice Farmington nodded vigorously.

"Yes, we've allowed you to talk at two meetings now, " she insisted. "This is not appropriate."

For Beth the spell was broken. Eloquence suddenly overtaken by anger. She had not even had a chance to lay out the proposals, as she had so carefully planned and rehearsed.

"'Allowed'?" she cried, looking around. "'Allowed'? You work for me! All of you."

"OK, OK," Mortensen banged the gavel. "I've heard enough. Thank you, Mrs. Southwick, for your input, but we're moving on now."

CHAPTER 18

"The liberty of the press is a blessing when we are inclined to write against others, and a calamity when we find ourselves overborne by the multitude of our assailants"
Samuel Johnson, Poet, Critic and Writer

WINTER 2008/2009

SUNBURY, NEW HAMPSHIRE

"I think you need to change the playing field," Finn advised, in what had now become frequent strategy phone calls. Talking with him always gave Beth confidence. While she still suffered from occasional panic attacks and wondered if she were achieving anything other than making a complete fool of herself, he managed to treat all governmental authority with totally consistent disdain.

He had watched the previous meeting on TV.

"The problem is," he went on. "If you're not yet in a position to assemble a crowd of supporters in the school board meeting room, every time you say something they don't like they'll just shut you up like they did last week."

"What alternative do you have in mind?" Beth asked.

"Try writing in the newspaper. Not just a letter, they can bury those in the middle of a whole bunch of others so that nobody will see it. You need to try to get a couple of Op-Ed pieces published. They get more prominent positioning and lots of people read those."

Beth remembered that she had read Finn's piece about vouchers months earlier.

"If I were you" Finn continued. "I'd drop in and have a chat with the Editor. He won't be thrilled to see you, he's in Mortensen's pocket. But it will be hard for him to turn you down, especially if he thinks you might be able to get word out, in other media, that he's denying free speech. The pieces need to be about seven hundred words, and one last thing, make sure you choose the title, or they will pick one for you that will distort your message."

Beth thought the plan made sense. Her work in PR meant that she had plenty of experience in writing. She thought it was entirely feasible that she could make her point more cogently in print, than she could in front of a microphone. Besides, the process of writing would help her to organize her thoughts.

She put in a call to the offices of the Sunbury News, and arranged a meeting with the Editor for the next day.

Al Keene had held the position of Editor for the previous two years. His predecessor had made what Keene considered the almost incomprehensibly stupid error of going head to head with Jim Mortensen's organization by having his reporters delve into the details of some no-bid paving contracts that had been issued by Mortensen's pals on the Town Council.

Although it wasn't public knowledge, Mortensen had subsequently paid a visit to the offices of the Sunbury News parent company in Massachusetts. There, he had not so subtly explained to the chief executive that he had connections to every major advertiser in the Sunbury News and that said advertising revenue would be reduced to perilously close to nothing at all unless a new Editor were in place within a week.

The CEO got the message, the previous Editor was reassigned to "special duties" elsewhere in the organization and Al Keene had found himself with a promotion.

Keene had been carefully following the recent activity regarding the schools. He had fielded several calls from Mortensen relating to how the Board Chairman would like to see the topic presented to the masses in Sunbury.

To say that he did not particularly welcome Beth's visit would have been an understatement. It put him in the tricky position of balancing the ethics of a free press with Keene's primary journalistic priority which was preserving his job.

As far as he was concerned, the only thing worse than having Mortensen gunning for him would be a loose cannon like Beth Southwick spouting off elsewhere that he was denying her access. Besides, she might be able to boost his dwindling circulation a bit. To cover himself, he checked with Massachusetts first. They said, "Yes." And Beth was in business as a social commentator.

Under the title "OWN GOAL", she had her first piece published after Christmas.

America is in the fight of its life. The battle is not taking place in the deserts of Iraq or a mountain pass in Afghanistan. Instead, it is occurring daily amid whirring machinery in the factories of China, India, Mexico, Pakistan and a host of other countries, where members of a practically unlimited workforce are willing to exchange a day of strenuous labor for fifteen dollars or less. Sometimes a lot less.

Frankly, we are not even fighting back.

The existence of an abundance of low wage labor will have a profound impact on the lives of too many of our children. All the worldwide military skirmishes put together are trivial in relation. Herein lies the real crisis for America. The Boeing 747, container ships, and the internet have combined to cause an explosion in the global availability of assembly workers, and to drive the value of unskilled labor into the toilet. That value will no longer support the American lifestyle.

For years we have papered over that imbalance with a mountain of debt. The recent financial crisis has proven that was not such a great idea for the long haul. We could probably paper it over again for a while with trade protectionism, there will certainly be calls for that defeatist band-aid in the coming months, but that would only create an even bigger dislocation later on.

The long term solution is straightforward. Although we don't want to admit it, the occupations that have made us prosperous in the past are now not worth nearly as much. So we must develop a post-industrial, much more highly skilled workforce that can add sufficient value, doing different sorts of jobs, to keep us in the manner to which we have become accustomed.

Politically incorrect or not, the reality is that we need more engineers and less wrench-turners, or we're heading straight into the same historical dustbin as all the other dominant societies who thought they'd remain on top forever.

The answer, clearly, begins and ends with education. If we are to triumph in the great international contests of the 21ˢᵗ century, it will be done not with bullets but with algebra books. After all, we can hardly go around nuking other countries for selling us automobiles too cheaply.

At present, we are approaching this battle with both hands tied behind our back. Our response so far has been to uphold, and even to glorify, the monopoly status of the nation's dismally ineffective public schools which graduate approximately five million students each year, fully half of whom can barely score a thousand on the combined math and verbal SAT.

Continuing our reliance on these schools and their methods will inevitably result in a catastrophic decline of wealth in America, and will, in turn, create one of history's greatest ironies. The nation that overwhelmed fascism, faced down communism, and, almost alone, had the spine to confront the new threat of global terrorism, will be brought to its knees by fatally underestimating the stringent demands of its very own creed of capitalism.

The initial reaction was modest.

There were a couple of letters in the next edition, from Mortensen's supporters, saying that it was about time Ms. Southwick left town if she didn't like the way things were. Beth was getting more and more used to that sort of message. It still stung, initially, to see her name dragged into the mud, but deeper down she was starting to believe the old saying that "all ink is good ink", and she welcomed the increased name recognition that even the harshest of letters conferred on her campaign.

A couple of days after the article was printed, however, she was in her car taking the kids home from the dentist. She was listening to a popular talk radio show from a station in Concord.

The host's name was Dan Fielding. He called his show "Fielding Questions".

"There was a very interesting Op-Ed piece in the Sunbury News this week, authored by a lady called Beth Southwick. I want to read it to you and then invite your comments."

Beth pulled the car over to the side of the road and listened as Fielding read her words over the air to thousands of listeners.

"Well," Fielding concluded. "Judging by the fact that my switchboard just lit up like a Christmas tree, Ms. Southwick has struck a bit of a nerve here. Let's get straight to our callers."

In another part of New Hampshire, Jim Mortensen, also in his car and tuned in to the same radio station, cringed. He knew how many people in Sunbury listened to Fielding's show.

"That moron Editor, printing this tripe," he yelled out. But he knew yelling wasn't going to help. Inside of him a worm was turning over and over. Beth Southwick was developing a following, and that could spell a lot of trouble for Jim Mortensen.

The first caller identified herself as an official with the teachers' union.

"I'm just fed up of all this teacher bashing, and horrified that you would condone it by reading out this hateful material on the air."

"Okay, Ma'am," interrupted Fielding. "But is Ms. Southwick correct, in your opinion? Does low achievement in our public schools pose a threat to our prosperity. And, if so, what should we do about it?"

The interruption flustered the caller.

"That's not the point," she stammered. "The point is that every time anything happens, the teachers always get the blame and someone who clearly knows nothing at all about education starts whining about test scores."

Fielding cut her off.

"Well. Personally I think what we just heard is a huge part of the problem. We just had a member of the monopoly of providers of public education calling, and she didn't even want to discuss whether or not there was a problem. Callers, let's stick to the question here. What the writer is saying is that we can't go back to where we were before. We are hopelessly uncompetitive in terms of cost when it comes to making commodity type products, and that therefore we need to teach the kids different things in school so that they are capable of higher value occupations. Next caller. John from the seacoast."

"Hi Dan, I just want to commend the writer for the content of her article. I think she's hit the nail on the head."

"Thank you, 'Sleepless on the Seacoast'," Beth murmured under her breath. She put the car in gear and drove on.

The debate wound on over the airwaves. Just as in Sunbury, it seemed that most of the people who were consumers of the system favored change. Most of the providers insisted that the status quo was not broken.

"But then again," Beth thought. "It's not their jobs that are being outsourced, is it?"

117

By the time her second article was printed in mid-January, Beth's name was becoming well known in Sunbury.

Beth had done her homework thoroughly. In December and January she had made a series of visits to the schools and the school district office to ask for information.

By now she was a known quantity, and her arrival was never greeted warmly. But she had discovered that most requests for data were, nevertheless, dealt with promptly. The last thing the school district wanted, since it was bound to lose, was to get hit with a "Public Right to Know" lawsuit.

Amongst the things she discovered were that the school district budget had risen from around $26 million in 1996 to over $65 million in 2009, while the enrollment had increased by only twenty-five percent and the consumer price index by about forty percent. If the budget had only increased in line with student numbers and inflation, it would be in the range of $45 million, not $65 million.

It was astonishing. In 1996, the expenditure was a little over six thousand dollars per student. Now it was thirteen thousand.

And what had all this spending purchased?

In 1996 average combined SAT scores were 1020, today they were exactly the same.

Perhaps most staggering of all were the Advanced Placement exams. From the results of the previous summer, she discovered that only eight Sunbury students had passed an AP examination. Four hundred students had graduated. Only one subject, calculus, was even offered in the curriculum. As trade became more and more global, it was not possible, at the supposedly cutting edge Sunbury High School, to study a foreign language to the level of Advanced Placement.

In the absence of school choice, she was as certain as she could be that the future prosperity of her state was going to be a direct function of the number of Advanced Placement examinations passed by high school students.

The public schools were not going to set aggressive performance targets for themselves. So she would try to set the goals, at least in Sunbury, for them.

In mid January she published her second article:

NO MORE BUILDINGS UNTIL RESULTS IMPROVE

In my last editorial, I argued that the manufacturing jobs that made America prosperous will inevitably continue to move off shore because of the availability of low wage labor overseas. If we want to maintain our living standards, and our status as an influential nation, we have no alternative but to redefine completely our notion of what constitutes an effective workforce. That, in turn, means that we must dramatically enhance what we expect our children to learn in school.

Twenty-five years ago, the infamous Bell Report warned of a "rising tide of mediocrity" in the public schools. Ever since, in response, we have poured money into those same schools at phenomenal rates to make ourselves feel good about our support of education.

We like to think, here in Sunbury, that, as a result of all our spending, we share no part of that mediocrity. We are constantly bombarded with school district propaganda, and report cards covered in A's, that attempts to convince us that we are the beneficiaries of a school system that is unparalleled in its successful delivery of education to our children.

Any rational analysis, however, leads to a different conclusion. All the expenditure has bought exactly and precisely nothing in terms of improved student achievement. We are a wealthy community where there are no pressing social problems to blame for low academic performance. Nevertheless, our children's test scores have stagnated at a level that is completely inconsistent with an expectation that they will find success and prosperity in the increasingly complicated global economy that confronts them.

It is time to try a new approach.

Fortunately for us, there is a yardstick readily available by which we can measure progress. The Advanced Placement Examinations, usually known as AP, are deemed by most observers as approximately equivalent to the stringent tests that students in countries that are our industrial competitors must pass to gain admission to college.

Seniors in the UK, for example, sit examinations called "A-levels", that equate in level of difficulty to our AP. Students there pass an average of approximately one 'A-level' examination per head of the population.

The sad fact is that last summer in Sunbury, with a graduating class of almost four hundred students, only eight AP examinations were passed. So, to generate an equivalent performance to the general population of the UK, we would have to raise our pass rate no less than fifty times higher than what we have today.

Today, once again, the school board is asking us to dig into our pockets to fund the latest planned addition to their real estate portfolio.

I call on the board and the administration to focus instead on developing a set of clearly stated achievement goals, along with a realistic plan to reach them. The target should be at least equivalent to what is expected of students completing secondary education in Britain, Germany, France and Japan.

It is futile to spend money on new school buildings if we have no plan for serious learning to occur once the structure is in place. My recommendation to the voters in this community is that, by our votes, we impose a moratorium on new construction until such time as we have a measurably world class instructional program in place.

The day after the article appeared in print Beth came out of her house to find her car on the driveway. Both rear tires were slashed clean through.

Beth had indeed struck a nerve. The Blob loved new buildings above all else. Challenging its previously unquestioned right to expand was not going to go unanswered. This time she had gone beyond the pale.

It did not exactly pour oil on troubled waters when Beth followed up in the next edition by questioning the second pillar of public school orthodoxy. She asked whether parents should have to accept a 'one size fits all' program, or should be allowed to select from a menu of pedagogical approaches.

WHY DOES EVERYTHING HAVE TO BE THE SAME IN OUR SCHOOLS?

The more I become involved with school district policy, the more it seems to me that there is a disturbing contradiction at the heart of the approach used to deliver instruction to our children.

If the goal of the district is really to cater to the best interests of the students, and not merely to maintain power and control, then it is hard for me as a parent to understand why more varieties of instruction are not made available.

The district exists to provide educational services to the children of the taxpayers of the community. As such we are the customers.

Whenever we go to a restaurant or to a car dealership in town, we are presented with choices as to which of a variety of products best meets our needs. But nothing like that happens with our school system. You pay your taxes, and whether you like it or not you get the 'Learning Through Discovery' program.

As I have talked to neighbors and parents all over town it seems to me that there is a fundamental difference of opinion over whether this educational approach is difficult enough to obtain the best efforts from our students.

I would in no way attempt to deny that there are a large number of parents who approve wholeheartedly of the instructional program. But the school district, on the other hand, seems determined to refuse to recognize that there are also substantial numbers, myself included, who yearn for a more traditional and rigorous approach.

In each grade of the elementary and middle schools we have approximately twenty classes operating at any given point of the day. Would it not make sense to switch some of those twenty, according to demand, to a different approach where students are prepared for the AP classes and examinations that I wrote about last week?

It wouldn't cost more. We would just be changing what is written on the blackboard in some classrooms, not adding new ones. No new teachers would be required.

Then parents could simply choose between traditional or discovery type learning, and more of the districts' taxpayers and customers would be able to feel good about the type of education their children are receiving.

We could then also abandon the debate about what is right and what is wrong, and all the acrimony that goes along with that, and just recognize that people think differently about what is best for their children.

It is sad, when you think of how much classroom time is spent at the moment lecturing our children about tolerance and respect, that the school district as a whole has so little forbearance towards anyone not willing to worship unconditionally at the altar of its educational philosophy.

The next edition of the Sunbury News might as well have been re-titled "The Case against Beth Southwick". Under the headline "Local Parent Blasts School Performance", board members, administrators and teachers practically had to take a number to get their quotes included.

Mortensen labeled her an ingrate for "hurling insults indiscriminately at hard working teachers", Superintendent Hamlin stuck with his usual "unfortunate remarks", and added that the school district was, "in constant review of the instructional program, using a research based process, to ensure that it meets best practice." Amidst the torrent of self-righteous outrage, neither of them addressed the issues of district test scores or of providing a choice.

Several parents had weighed in too, expressing gratitude for the "caring approach" that the school district had lavished upon their children, and therefore denying the need for any other option.

"Hardly the point," Beth thought, wondering whether they had actually read what she had written.

Editor Al Keene had made sure that not a single supportive voice was included in the article. Even handedness could only be taken so far.

In his office, Keene sat back in his chair and smiled. By giving old man Mortensen an opportunity to get in a few good licks in return, it had all turned out better than he had expected. The edition had sold out from the vending machines, but he had managed to get an emergency second print run. All indications were that the issue would set a record for distribution. Head office would love it. What was even better was that the story had "legs". He could milk this one for months as long as Beth Southwick didn't panic and fold the tent.

CHAPTER 19

"All the candidates…they all know each other, they all move in the same circles, and
what I'm doing is breaking into the country club."
Howard Dean, Doctor and Politician

FEBRUARY 2009

SUNBURY, NEW HAMPSHIRE

"'Worship at the altar', indeed!" Bob Finn had called her.

"Yes, I wondered if that was a bit over the top," Beth conceded. "But I couldn't
resist it."

"Listen, Beth, have you given any thought to the election?"

The annual school district election was held in mid-March. The filing deadline was
rapidly approaching.

"Some, yes. Why, what are you thinking?"

"You have to run for the board now," he said. "You have the most name recognition
of anyone in Sunbury."

"Yeah, that's supposed to be a good thing, right? So far all it's got me are two
wrecked tires," Beth recounted what had happened to her car.

"That's awful! My God, they must be getting desperate. Do you think you could get
a running mate, by the way?"

"No," Beth chuckled. "After what's happened to me I hardly feel comfortable
inviting anyone else to join in. Why would I need one?"

"There are two seats. Mortensen's machine will undoubtedly put up two candidates.
Probably the incumbents, Farmington and Reddington. Here's your problem.
Suppose on election day a thousand of Mortensen's toadies show up. Nearly all one
thousand will vote for both of those guys, because they're the same thing so there's
no reason to vote for one and not the other."

"Well then," interrupted Beth, puzzled. "All I have to do is get twelve hundred and
I'm okay."

"Not so fast," countered Finn. "Think about the second vote."

"What about it?"

"Everyone coming into the booth gets two votes not just one. Suppose your twelve
hundred supporters arrive, and put a mark next to your name. But then they split their

second vote evenly between Alice and John, not because they like Alice and John but because the ballot tells them to vote for 'Not more than two' and there's no other choice. Then, adding that six hundred each to the thousand they got from their own supporters, they each end up with sixteen hundred to your twelve hundred."

"Oh," pondered Beth, with reality dawning slowly that a two against one fight for two seats was going to make things almost impossibly difficult for her. "Is that what 'bullet' voting is all about? I never really understood it before now."

"Precisely," Finn confirmed. "Very few people do understand it. But it's critical. You have to get out the message to your supporters that they should only make one vote not two, otherwise they help the other side. In the example we just discussed, you end up losing an election that you actually got more supporters to attend."

"Perhaps I shouldn't run then, after all, if I'm just going to get clobbered. Unless, of course, you want to run as well. It sounds like together we have a much better chance."

"I'd love to help, Beth, but I'm out of town too often to make all the meetings." It seemed that there were limits, even for Bob Finn.

"You should run anyway, " Finn went on. "It gives you the forum that you need. But I have another idea."

"Go on," said Beth.

"Well, you've lit a fire with your suggestions about student performance. If you run and lose, because you're in a two against one, Mortensen's mob will portray it as rejection of your ideas. So you should put something on the ballot that's a referendum on your proposals."

"I'm allowed to do that?"

"Yes," said Finn. "In New Hampshire it's really easy to get questions on the ballot for school district elections. All you have to do is get twenty-five signatures of registered voters on a piece of paper and the district has to include the question."

"Really? And if it passes they then have to implement?"

"Well, I have to admit, that's Catch 22," Finn cautioned. "Citizen petition votes are 'advisory only' to the board. Frankly, they would probably ignore you. But that gives you a tremendous moral superiority for anything else you decide to do. Voters hate having their expressed will overturned by bureaucrats. It would almost be the best thing that could happen. You could make Mortensen's life miserable without having the inconvenience of having to spend hours and hours at board meetings."

"So, if we did that," Beth concluded. "There would actually be three things on the ballot, right? A vote for school board, a vote for the new building, and a vote for performance based goal setting."

"That's right. Since the building vote involves bonding, it requires a super-majority vote of sixty percent to pass. There's a good chance that will fail anyway with the economy being as bad as it is. So it's a good one to link to your proposal, that way, if the building fails, you can make it look like the community has supported your moratorium. Your petition would require only a simple majority to pass. And since it sounds reasonable and doesn't involve spending money it has a good chance of passing. Even if you don't get elected to the board you could win two out of three and put yourself in a strong position."

"Sounds like a plan to me," Beth agreed. "How do I get the twenty-five signatures for the petition?"

"Already done," laughed Finn. "I passed a paper round at the taxpayer association meeting last night. Every single person there signed it. I think you should submit it though. Oh, and one other thing, if you're going to be a politician in New Hampshire, get a pair of warm boots."

The next day, Beth Southwick became a candidate for the school board.

It was remarkably easy. She went to the house of the school district clerk, signed a form and handed over the registration fee. One dollar.

She had no idea whether she would get elected to the school board. In fact she was far from sure that she wanted to be. Every now and again William Buckley's words came back to her. The great raconteur and essayist had once run for mayor of New York as a way of propagating his conservative message. When asked what he would do on his first day in office if he happened to win, Buckley had replied, "Demand a recount."

She was beginning to understand that winning elections was not necessarily the only reason to become a candidate. The forum that a candidacy provided allowed for an enhanced impact of the drip feed process that Finn had described to her. William Jennings Bryan, she knew, had lost on all three occasions that he had been nominated for President by the Democratic party. Yet many of the policy initiatives he pursued, such as the federal income tax, women's suffrage, a Department of Labor, and currency reform were now, for better or worse, unquestioned staples of the American way of life.

She also submitted the petition that Finn had dropped off at her home. The question read, "Shall the school district define and pursue an aggressive set of academic performance goals, based on independently graded Advanced Placement Examinations, that are at least equivalent to average performance of students resident in the nations that are major industrial competitors of the United States. To achieve said goals, shall the district provide all parents of students in the elementary and middle schools the option of choosing classrooms offering traditional and rigorous instructional programs that are not connected to the Learning Through Discovery plan."

Five minutes after Beth left the clerk's house, the phone rang on the desk of Jim Mortensen's office.

"Yes," Mortensen answered in the bored tone that was designed to indicate to any caller that Mortensen had more pressing business to attend to.

It was Courmeyer on the other end of the line. The clerk, part of the Mortensen network, had reported to him what had just occurred. Courmeyer, as one of Mortensen's first lieutenants, had the unenviable task of delivering the news to the boss.

"Well, what the Hell did you expect?" snapped Mortensen. Actually, he had assumed that Beth wouldn't have the guts to run. Especially after the little incident with the tires. But he still needed to convey to Courmeyer that the Great Mortensen was always two steps ahead of everyone else in political clairvoyance.

"There's something else, too, Jim."

"Go on," a foreboding came over Mortensen. Courmeyer read the petition.

"Oh, for God's sake. What does that mean?" He banged down the phone.

He knew that Bob Finn and Beth Southwick had found the weak spot in the armor of the school district monopoly. They were asking the electorate if they would like something for nothing.

CHAPTER 20

"We were told our campaign wasn't sufficiently slick. We regard that as a compliment."

Margaret Thatcher, British Politician and Prime Minister

FEBRUARY 2009

SUNBURY, NEW HAMPSHIRE

With an assist from Bob Finn, Beth Southwick took a crash course in Election 101.

"First of all,' he told her. "You need a video. Masses of people watch the Citizen Access channel. Most of the folks in the studio are in Mortensen's army, but I'm registered as a user. I'll borrow a camera and reserve some time for a shoot. Just put together a script with your message. If you have some charts – test scores and stuff like that, bring those along too. We'll edit them in."

Beth had enjoyed making the video. Douglas helped her carry an armchair into the studio, and she sat in front of a curtain doing a sort of "fireside chat" while Finn rolled the camera.

She explained her rationale for running for the board. That she believed that the students were capable of greater achievement levels if only the expectation were placed on them, and parents were given more choices. She urged a new political dimension: that, this time, the school district should put forward plans for performance improvement before any new buildings or major budget increases were approved. She used charts of test scores to show how all the recent expenditure increases, both locally and statewide, had produced nothing of value educationally.

Finn took the footage and edited it into what Beth thought looked like a highly professional program. She was quite surprised that within a couple of days of initiating the video project they could have an effective product ready to go out on the air.

Finn delivered the program to the media center director. Like everything else in Sunbury, the center was staffed by town employees who owed their position to an appointment by Jim Mortensen's group. The director took one look at the content of Finn's tape and called her patron.

The optimal time for the video to show, they both knew, was around ten in the evening, when local people would be channel surfing before going to bed.

"Put it on at four in the afternoon," Mortensen ordered. The schedule ran the same programs each day for a week unless there was some local special event that required live coverage. "And make sure that it gets pre-empted by High School basketball at every available opportunity."

Then there were her signs, planted all over town in the snow banks in front yards and next to businesses. Finn had provided her with a list of supporters, accumulated over years of political involvement, who would host signs. Some had premium spots on corner lots. She had blistered her hands hammering in stakes. Once again Finn had come to the rescue. Having participated in winter time elections for years, he owned a special metal spike tool that could more easily pierce the frozen New Hampshire tundra and make a pilot hole for the wooden tomato stake that bore the sign.

She had spent some time thinking about the message to display. In the end she went with a bright red sign with her name and a check mark next to it. Underneath, the sign bore her slogan; "Accountability First: Buildings Second".

A number of her signs were destroyed. Several of them were knocked over and the stakes splintered. Nearby, there were tire tracks in the snow that looked remarkably similar in each case. One sign was even burnt. The perpetrator had gone to the trouble of building and igniting a small bonfire around the stake. As far as she could tell, none of the signs for Alice Farmington or John Reddington had received similar treatment.

The barrage of negative publicity in the local paper was unabated.

The teachers had clearly organized to ensure that every edition of the paper had at least two letters explaining how the new facility was vital in order to continue the tradition of excellence which, they claimed, had become synonymous with the Sunbury program. Some of the letters bore simple grammatical errors.

"Anti-child" was another label the opponents sought to pin on her.

Beth shook her head at that one.

"How can encouraging students to learn more math be 'anti-child'," she wondered.

Her proposals to reduce reliance on mixed ability classes had been a lightning rod. The "E-word" had emerged, with writers branding her as "elitist" in several letters.

She had expected that there would be a barrage of criticism in that direction at the annual candidates' debate, and she was not disappointed. The debate, too, was organized and moderated by the "Friends of Jim Mortensen".

The debate took place in the high school auditorium, and was broadcast on the community TV station. Each candidate was given five minutes to speak. Beth reprised a lot of the material from her video, mentioning specific goals for AP passes. She showed charts of current test scores, flat or declining, and superimposed other graphs of the district budget heading upwards at a rate far greater than inflation and student enrollment combined. Finally, she showed some examples of the endless cut and paste activities that permeated the first grade classroom that her own son attended. She closed with an appeal for more opportunities for parents to select rigorous programs. Her presentation was greeted with a deafening silence broken finally by three claps of applause from Douglas. A handful of other folks joined in. Ying Chang was there. Beth smiled at them.

She was followed at the podium by Alice Farmington who, not surprisingly presented a different view of the world. She lectured on how the "glory of the public schools" was the equal opportunity concept of "high standards for all, not just a select few." If re-elected to the board she would, she promised, "re-double her efforts to make sure that the outstanding faculty had all the tools and facilities that they needed to continue the tradition of excellence for which Sunbury education is justifiably known."

Before she even finished her peroration, the assembled crowd, many of whom Beth recognized as being the same teachers who had attended the board meeting at which she had been so resoundingly battered, was on its feet cheering and applauding. Alice Farmington could take plenty of that. She waved as if she had just been nominated for president.

Next up was John Reddington. He might as well have just said, "Ditto", and sat down. Beth caught Jim Mortensen in the audience, yawning. He looked up and saw that she had noticed. A moment of mutual understanding passed between them, they grinned at each other, both silently acknowledging that John Reddington was a moron.

"Strange," thought Beth. "I can't stand him, and he can't stand me, but we both recognize that there is an element of sport in all of this."

The applause was less enthusiastic when Reddington wound up, but still a marked improvement on what had greeted the end of Beth's remarks.

The moderator, another Mortensen-picked operative named Rod Weiss, moved to the microphone. Ron Courmeyer was already on his feet in the audience.

"Yes, Ron?"

Courmeyer looked embarrassed.

"Oh, I just wanted to be sure I got a chance to ask a question."

"Well, I'll be sure that we get to you. If you wouldn't mind giving me just a minute to explain the rules of what's going to happen next."

Courmeyer flushed and sat down. Beth saw him anxiously look over towards Mortensen to get some sense of how badly he had screwed up. Courmeyer incorrectly perceived Weiss as an opponent in the Mortensen hierarchy. Looking stupid wasn't good for Courmeyer's promotion prospects.

Weiss was an unusual individual in the Sunbury political world in that he was relatively independent. By profession he was an investment banker, and had that suave confident manner about him that suggested personal financial wherewithal. He aligned with Mortensen's group only to gain access and involvement with the political scene in Sunbury, but he wasn't desperate, like some of the others, for public office or acclaim.

Mortensen recognized that Weiss' smooth exterior could be an asset, and used him for occasions like this when at least an aura of impartiality was required. "Better than bumpkins like Courmeyer and Reddington," he thought.

Weiss looked down at his notes.

"I'd like to thank all the candidates for their presentations," he said. "We have some fascinating differences of opinion this year, which I am sure will stimulate some thought provoking questions. For the next section of the evening, members of the audience are free to direct questions to one particular candidate or to all three. All I would ask is that we try to balance out the questions between the candidates as much as possible. Also, if a candidate would like to add some comments to an answer given by another candidate, then they should indicate that to me, and, as moderator, I'll try to give them some time. Is that okay with everyone?"

He looked around. All three candidates nodded.

"Right Ron," announced Weiss. "Fire away." There was just a hint of condescension in it.

Courmeyer was a large man. He puffed himself up to his full height, and set out to make amends for appearing foolish.

"I have a question for Ms. Southwick." There was a gladiatorial tone to his voice, as if he were challenging her to a duel.

Beth smiled at him. Her presentation had gone well. She was confident. She was also fairly certain that she knew what the question was going to be.

"Ms. Southwick," it was almost a sneer. "You have stated in your video, your articles, and in your presentation tonight, that you believe parents should be able to select rigorous courses for their children. Shouldn't we expect high standards for all students. Won't your proposal create an elite group and be highly divisive?"

Beth was ready.

"Oh, sort of like the high school football team, you mean?" she inquired innocently. Courmeyer was still on his feet. Ying Chang burst out laughing in the back row. Courmeyer looked around angrily and sat down.

Beth adjusted the microphone. There was no trembling in her hands. This was going to be like Margaret Thatcher during Prime Minister's question time in the British House of Commons. She was going to clock this one clean out of the park.

"The funny thing is, Mr. Courmeyer, I could swear that I have heard that, during the late summer, you can be seen out on the fields with a clipboard during football tryouts. Now your son, as I understand it, is a gifted wide receiver who makes the team easily. But the rest of the kids require careful vetting by you, to make sure they meet your exacting standards, before they are allowed to join him on the program.

"Tell me, Mr. Courmeyer, during the week of the Concord game, do we put up a sign-up sheet in the hallway so that 'all' the children have an opportunity to enjoy the thrill of taking a couple of snaps at quarterback in the big game?

"No, no, no, we do not. Only the fleet of foot and strong of arm get to go where your son treads, isn't that the case, Mr. Courmeyer?"

It had gone very quiet.

"So forgive me, Mr. Courmeyer, if I decline to accept the concept that I need a 'holier-than-thou' lecture from you on the egalitarian nature of public education."

Ying Chang laughed again. Then everyone else did too. Except Ron Courmeyer.

Beth went on.

"One thing I have learned for certain, and perhaps it's the only thing I'm certain of, is that we all think differently about what constitutes a good education for our children. That's why it is so important to abandon the search for a single perfect curriculum and allow a variety of choices instead.

"I think, by now, everyone knows that I favor the presentation of much more rigorous material to children at a much earlier age. But, I'm sure that there are other parents who like the Learning Through Discovery program in the elementaries, and think that discovery learning is a great thing.

"If they think that, then there's no reason why they should have to have their children educated according to what I think. Similarly though, no parent who believes that the Discovery Program represents nothing more than crass dumbing down should have it inflicted on their children.

"We don't have to have the debate about who's right and who's wrong. We just need to provide the choices and let parents decide for themselves.

"There is no contradiction here in my proposals with the principle of equal opportunity for anyone participating in public education. Unfortunately, we get mixed up with the difference between equal opportunity and equal outcome. In education, equal opportunity means that we should give every student the chance to acquire as many skills and capabilities, and as much knowledge as his or her individual motivation and talent will allow. Just because such a policy would result in wildly different outcomes does not make it unfair in any way, shape or form."

Beth was enjoying herself enormously. The room was completely silent. She was reciting all of the one-liners that, over the past few weeks, she had come to recognize had the most effect on those she spoke to. She felt completely in control.

She was quite surprised that Weiss hadn't stopped her on grounds of time limits. But she saw he was listening intently too, and seemed to have temporarily forgotten his role in that regard. Out of the corner of her eye she could see Mortensen trying, as unobtrusively as possible, to catch his attention.

Since they weren't going to stop her, she would carry on.

"What we must not continue, because it is desperately unfair to the students as individuals and is also absurd public policy for a post-industrial society, is the present practice of allowing the army to march at the pace of the slowest. That is what we are achieving through our policy of relying on mixed ability classrooms and failing to set clearly defined academic goals for the system as a whole.

"That's a major plank of my platform. As long as we have no performance goals, no performance is precisely what we are going to get."

There was a rumble of discontent from the audience.

"If we want to be achieving at a level comparable to the schools of our industrial competitors in developed nations around the world, then, here in Sunbury, we should be obtaining four or five hundred passes in Advanced Placement examinations each year. Would anyone care to guess at how many we achieved last year?"

She looked around the room. There was no answer.

"Eight," she said. "Not eight hundred. Eight."

"And yet we've just heard Alice, in her presentation, claim victory and receive a 'standing O'."

"I find it quite interesting that there are so many teachers and administrators in the audience here tonight, and, judging by applause levels, they are all firmly committed to keeping the incumbents on the board who will ask very little of them.

"There is something wrong with that. The board is supposed to represent the interests of the students and taxpayers, not the faculty. Those interests are represented by low taxes and high achievement levels. If things were the right way around, the board would be demanding those and the faculty would be objecting loudly that too much is being expected of them."

She looked straight into the TV camera that was positioned in the central aisle.

"If I'm elected, I promise that I will never forget precisely who it is that I am working for. I will push for the goal of four hundred AP passes per year, within eight years, to become the central focus of the work of the board. I don't believe that we need any new buildings or tax increases to accomplish that. What we need is a plan to ensure that the colored pencils are put away when Art class is over, and meaningful curriculum content is delivered daily to every child whose family chooses to participate."

She paused, it was silent again.

"So Mr. Courmeyer, don't get me wrong. I support the concept of your football team. To me, it makes perfect sense that talented football players are grouped with other players of like capability, as long as everyone else is also given an opportunity

131

to play and improve at whatever level of interest and skills they possess. We set high standards for football. We assess the opposition and do what we have to do in order to win. As a result, most of the time it seems, we do win."

"I just want to do the exact same thing for academics. Maybe you'd like to work with me on that? Bring your clipboard."

The silence lasted for two beats.

Ying Chang stood and clapped. She was followed by Douglas, Chloe and Bob Finn. The scattered applause echoed in staccato fashion around the room. The teachers looked on sullenly.

Beth had a sudden sense that this was the high water mark of her entire effort and she should quit while she was ahead.

She looked over to Weiss, the moderator.

"Mr. Moderator, I am sure I have handily exceeded my share of the allotted time, and, in all honesty, I have said everything I know that pertains to my campaign. So I think I'll leave the rest of the session to my opponents."

She stood and extended a hand to Farmington and Reddington in turn. Looking a little shell shocked, each of them shook hands.

She leaned forward to the portly Reddington and whispered, "You should also teach the boys to stand when they shake hands with a lady."

Then she turned on her heel and left the room.

CHAPTER 21

"Ninety percent of the politicians give the other ten percent a bad name."
Henry Kissinger, Statesman

MARCH 2009

POLLING PLACE, SUNBURY, NEW HAMPSHIRE

"God bless you for what you are doing."

The woman who had approached Beth in the middle of the afternoon, was probably almost eighty years old.

"That was you on the TV, wasn't it?" she had asked.

"Yes," Beth had replied. "I made a program."

"I read your articles too," the woman said. "It takes a lot of courage to do what you have taken on. All those awful things they've written about you. Just for asking questions and looking out for the kids, so they can learn properly."

The old lady paused, shaking her head. Then she patted Beth on the arm.

"Thank you dear, this community is in your debt, whatever anyone says. Don't forget that."

Hours later, the comment was still warming Beth's heart, but her feet were frozen. She had thought Finn's advice about warm boots was a joke, but after standing outside the polls for twelve straight hours, she now fully understood what he meant.

It took a hardy physique in addition to a well honed political message to compete in elections in New Hampshire.

The polls were in the High School Gymnasium. The main High School parking lot had been reserved for the day for voters. A set of waist high barricades was positioned at the edge of the lot, adjacent to the doorway of the building. Next to the barricades, tied on with string, or stuck in the snow that still lay on the grass, a forest of political signs on tomato stakes urged support of one candidate or another. Since anyone holding signs and advocating for a candidate had to remain behind the barricades, that meant standing on snow if you wanted to press your cause. Beth had lost all sensation in her toes several hours ago.

A sense of elation was coming over her. Not that she was certain that she had won. Far from it, in fact. But she knew that she had given a good account of herself and her message. Enough people had approached her during the day with supportive comments that, even if she hadn't achieved a majority, it was patently clear that her message had got through to the community.

It had been dark for over an hour, the last few stragglers rushed from their cars to cast a vote before the polls closed.

Beth shouted the message she had been urging all day, "Southwick for school board, 'Yes' on twelve, 'No' to the bond." Article twelve was her citizen's petition on setting goals for AP exam results. The bond was the school board's article requesting funding for the new elementary school.

But, in contrast to earlier in the day when daylight had let the voters see who was delivering the message, and a shake of the head or a thumbs up in response allowed Beth to do her own informal polling, now there was little to indicate which way the last minute vote was going.

The district moderator appeared at the Gymnasium door.

"Last call for voters," he yelled. "Anyone else want to vote? The polls are closing in one minute. One more minute."

A final member of the electorate came running in from the side of the parking lot. Douglas was positioned there.

"Southwick for School Board," he yelled.

"Squat and rotate, buddy," came the answer. Douglas didn't hear properly, and gave the guy a cheery wave.

"Did you hear what he said?" Beth asked, walking up.

"No."

She explained. He laughed.

"Hope that's not a metaphor for the whole campaign!"

Not much more she could do now. Suddenly weary, she leaned on the barricade and closed her eyes momentarily. The pile of flyers that she had been passing out to voters dropped to the snow. Douglas picked them up, and gave her a hug.

"I'm proud of what you did, whatever the outcome," he said. "It's funny. I'll be happy if you win, and I'll be happy if you lose."

She knew exactly what he meant. She felt the same way.

It had been an experience that she would not have missed for the world. But it was undeniable that it had put a strain on her family. It was very difficult, she had discovered, to participate in politics at anything other than 'warp speed'. Once you were 'in' it grabbed hold of your psyche and crowded out all other thoughts. She actually understood now, the emotions that led someone like Jim Mortensen to become what he had. She guessed that he had started out with a view to making things work better, but, along the way, the lure of power and control had got in the way. 'Who rode the tiger could never dismount'. Could that be a place that she could end up in if she won?

"Douglas?"

"What?"

"Don't ever let me lose sight of what we're battling for, or the fact that you and the kids are more important than all of this."

"Tricky problem, isn't it?" he said. "You're trying to do the right thing for our kids, but in order to do so you have to devote all your efforts to something other than them. The system's big and it's broken, Beth, I think it's going to take more than just you to fix it."

They meandered over to their car and dropped off the flyers and the signs.

"Well, no one could say I didn't try," she said. Now that it was done, there was almost a wave of nostalgia flowing over her.

"No, they couldn't," Douglas agreed.

The results would be announced about thirty minutes after the polls closed. She took his hand. They walked together into the gym to hear the verdict.

CHAPTER 22

"At the bottom of all the tributes paid to democracy is the little man, walking into the little booth, with a little pencil, making a little cross on a little bit of paper. . . ."
Winston Churchill, British Politician and Prime Minister

MARCH 2009

HIGH SCHOOL GYMNASIUM, SUNBURY, NEW HAMPSHIRE

There were perhaps two hundred people in the gym waiting to hear the results. All the local politicos were there as well as the school district lobby of teachers and administrators.

The vote counting machines had been moved to a small roped off area. The district moderator, a local lawyer, was scuttling around with pieces of paper tape and a calculator. He was scribbling totals on the back of an envelope.

Several among the crowd cast glances at Beth as she walked in with Douglas. But it was difficult for her to find a friendly face. So she just stood with Douglas. After a few minutes Bob Finn showed up with Chloe Roberts.

"How do you think it went? Do you think you picked up many bullet votes?" he asked.

"I thought it was good in general. But I'm not sure about the bullet votes. Lots of folks don't seem to understand that, and when they're just heading into the polls you can't do much more than ask them to vote for you," she said. "A lot of people definitely knew who I was, though."

"You think?" laughed Finn. "You're famous, Beth. I just wish you'd had a running mate, you would've clobbered the bastards. Anyway, we'll see. Good luck, you made one hell of an effort."

He turned to talk to Chloe.

"He thinks I've lost then," Beth whispered to Douglas.

The moderator moved to the edge of his little secure area by the voting machines.

"Can I have your attention, please," he had to shout to be heard over the buzz in the room. "I have the preliminary results."

Just like that, two hundred people were completely silent. The tension level went up a few notches. Beth could feel her heart pounding.

The moderator began.

"Article 1. Election of School Board members. Alice Farmington, two thousand, four hundred and thirty-two."

A shriek went up from the crowd. Beth looked around to see lots of people hugging each other. She felt like throwing up.

"John Reddington," the moderator intoned. "Two thousand, two hundred and eighty-four."

There was another, smaller, cheer.

"Elizabeth Southwick. Two thousand and seventy-seven. Alice Farmington and John Reddington are duly elected to three year terms on the school board."

There was a murmur of satisfaction. Beth had the adrenalin surging round her system. She wasn't even quite sure what the numbers were that had been read out.

Douglas hugged her and whispered something about bad luck. Over his shoulder Beth could see scenes of wild jubilation. Only one person looked unhappy. It was Jim Mortensen. He had done the math and knew what was coming.

Finn rushed up. Probably only he and Mortensen, in the whole room, fully understood the impact of the "two against one" situation and the lack of bullet voting.

"Bloody hell, Beth. You killed them," yelled Finn.

"What do you mean," asked Douglas. "She wasn't elected."

"Oh, but she won all right," Finn was almost beside himself with excitement. "Look, the other two only got a couple of hundred votes more each. But each of them will have picked up a thousand or so from second votes from the two thousand folks who came here for Beth but had nowhere else to put their second mark. This election was really twenty one hundred to fourteen hundred in your favor. Let's just wait and see how the rest comes out."

The moderator continued.

"Article 2. Shall the school district bond the amount of eleven million, four hundred thousand dollars for the purpose of construction of a new elementary school. This article requires a sixty percent supermajority for passage. Yeas, one thousand five hundred …"

The rest of the announcement was drowned by the huge groan that went up from the assembled crowd. Several very hostile glances were shot in Beth's direction.

"Nays: two thousand and twelve. Article two, the bond for the elementary school fails."

It had not even come close to achieving a simple majority let alone the sixty percent required. Finn was practically jumping up and down.

"That'll show the bastards" he was chuckling.

The moderator read on. The operating budget passed, and the janitors got a new contract passed. Beth heard something to do with Federal money for school lunches get approved, but it was all a bit of a blur.

"Article 12, by citizens petition. Shall the school district define and pursue an aggressive set of academic performance goals, based on independently graded Advanced Placement Examinations, that are at least equivalent to average performance of students resident in the nations that are major industrial competitors of the United States. To achieve said goals, shall the district provide all parents of students in the elementary and middle schools the option of choosing classrooms offering traditional and rigorous instructional programs that are not connected to the Learning Through Discovery plan."

He paused, adjusting his spectacles.

"Yeas, two thousand one hundred and sixteen, Nays, fourteen hundred and twenty. Article twelve passes."

The joy from the crowd that had greeted the election of their favored board members had now turned to outright despondency.

"Told you so," Finn beamed at her. "C'mon, lets go and celebrate."

Near the door, as they were walking out, Joan Simons, the Union president, approached them. The look on her face was one of pure hatred.

"I hope you're satisfied with what you've done," she practically spat the words out. "What a hateful thing. Here we are killing ourselves, every day, for your children, and you go out of your way to put roadblocks in the path of progress."

Beth was completely calm.

"Well, Ms. Simons, I suppose it all depends on the meaning of the word 'progress'. You maybe can't see it from here, but outside of these walls the world is a different place today, as much as you and I both wish it wasn't."

CHAPTER 23

"If Columbus had an advisory committee he would probably still be at the dock."
Arthur Goldberg, Supreme Court Justice

MARCH 2009

HIGH SCHOOL, SUNBURY, NEW HAMPSHIRE

Jim Mortensen, Alice Farmington, John Reddington and Superintendent Hamlin sat together in a classroom adjacent to the gymnasium where the election results had just been read.

The meeting was not legal. A majority of a public board should not meet together in private. Mortensen didn't care. Farmington and John Reddington didn't know. Hamlin knew, but just did as he was told.

The atmosphere was a strange one. Alice and John were still flushed with the adrenalin rush associated with having just won public office. Hamlin, too, was in good spirits. Even if he caught some of the blame for the lack of support for the new building, the makeup of the board probably meant that his job was secure for at least another couple of years.

Mortensen, however, was in a foul mood. He was keenly aware that a shift had taken place in town and it was not good for him. He was due to run for re-election next year. Since his was the only seat available then, he stood no chance of getting a two against one situation that had so obviously benefited this year's winners.

He was in a tricky spot. If he acceded to Article 12, the citizens' demand for accountability, he would lose support from the union. On the other hand if he ignored it, then Beth Southwick, or some other little bitch just like her, would crucify him for disregarding the voters. His ego could not stand a defeat at the polls.

"I just can't understand how the bond vote failed," Alice wittered, looking for something to break the awkward silence. "When John and I won comfortably."

"Oh, shut up," exploded Mortensen. "That's not the issue."

There was another silence. Even at times like this with hardly anyone watching, Mortensen couldn't resist the melodramatic.

"The issue," he said, as if explaining something patiently to a three year old. "Is what to do about the citizen petition article."

Reddington sighed.

"Well, since the law says it's advisory only, I say we should just dismiss it out of hand. We can say we don't have the resources to implement it and it would cost a fortune. That should get the taxpayers off our back"

"Brilliant," Mortensen replied sarcastically. "Just brilliant. But then again, you don't have to face the voters next year do you."

"Here's what we're going to do. What we always do. We'll stall. Superintendent Hamlin, I want you to set up a committee. It should comprise a majority of teachers and folks that we know for absolute certain are on our side. Put a couple of parents on there too."

"Mrs. Southwick?" inquired Hamlin.

"Jesus Christ, of course not, you idiot!" Mortensen was incredulous.

"I want to be certain," he went on. "That this committee never achieves a single damn thing."

AFTERMATH
"Any coward can fight a battle when he's sure of winning…..there are many
victories worse than a defeat."
George Eliot, Novelist

Jim Mortensen got his wish. The committee was created and embarked on a prolonged study of the AP program and program choice. By the following March it had still not published any results or conclusions. In fact it never did, nor did any school board member ever attend a meeting. Attendance dwindled and the committee quietly disbanded about a year later.

Mortensen continued to chair boards and committees in Sunbury for another ten years. Alice Farmington and John Reddington backed him up with reliable votes in support of whatever Jim Mortensen wanted.

Superintendent Hamlin retired from the Sunbury school district several years later with all the pension benefits that his adroit political maneuvering had accrued to him. He became an educational consultant, receiving plenty of handsomely compensated assignments from his carefully cultivated network of school officials around the state. Mostly, his consulting work involved finding ways for school districts to lower standards and expectations on students while producing sophisticated sounding reports and pronouncements claiming that the exact opposite was happening.

Pam Jackson remained active on just about every PTA committee and association in Sunbury. She also began to travel to other communities to speak in support of expanded funding for public schools. Eventually, with the help of state representative Bill Holmes, who visited the governor to trumpet her 'invaluable contributions', she was appointed to the New Hampshire Board of Education. With the status of her new position, she was able to accept occasional consulting contracts passed to her by Miles Hamlin when he thought the billing rate offered for the assignment was beneath his dignity.

Bob Finn maintained his drip feed approach to Sunbury local politics, writing Op-Eds in the Sunbury News and supporting candidates who came along every now and again to take a tilt at the status quo windmill. He never ran for office.

Ying Chang home-schooled her children. One of them subsequently attended Yale.

Bailey Hutchins, who had employed an Indian to write a fine college admission essay for him, duly surprised his professors by failing to generate similar quality work when left to his own devices. He never obtained a degree. Arunkhumar Patel, who wrote that essay while researching business opportunities in Bangalore, made a fortune. He eventually persuaded financial backers to help him open a clinic that performed hip replacements at a fraction of the cost for Americans, and with none of the waiting periods for Europeans, that his customers experienced in hospitals in their own countries.

The election had taught Beth Southwick a fundamental truth of school politics: that people are far more willing to support real reforms in the privacy of a voting booth than they are in front of a TV camera at a public meeting. She had polled over two thousand votes, yet, while she was berated by legions of hostile opponents, only a handful of supporters had shown up at board meetings or the candidates debate. Beth decided that local politics was an experience well worth doing once, but that she neither wanted to have her brains beaten out repeatedly nor could stomach the alternative, which was to sell her soul and become like Jim Mortensen.

It would take far more than a lone crusader, Beth realized, to generate the sort of seismic shift in policy that she was looking for.

She could take her place in the long line of reformers who had nudged the line a tiny bit. But she suspected that full fledged change would not come until such time as economic decline was linked to the shortcomings of a monopoly education system in the public's mind. That degree of leadership would take a courageous governor or presidential candidate. She couldn't see such a figure on the political horizon.

In Sunbury, though, even without her active involvement, her legacy lived on. Parents, some of them anyway, had taken notice of what Beth had had to say. Around town, the words "AP Exam" were typed into the Google search box on hundreds of computers. What the searchers found was that AP was a growing phenomenon. Other people's kids in other states were passing these exams at a much higher rate than students in New Hampshire. And there was a reason.

Many parents realized that if their kids could pass a few AP exams, and gain college credit, it would be possible to graduate in three years instead of four. Huge financial savings were possible. Quietly, but with increasing frequency and persuasiveness, they brought up the topic of availability of AP classes with teachers, principals and guidance counselors.

Over time, the school system got the message. There was to be no great revolution of the sort Beth had envisioned. No formal goal setting that would lead to a confrontation between the board and the educators. No admission of failure, or public recognition for the need for a U-turn in policy. But positions softened. Each year, in response to parental cajoling, one or two more AP classes appeared in the high school.

A decade or so later, around the time that Mike Southwick graduated, the annual number of AP exam passes in Sunbury rose to one hundred and fifty, from just eight in the year of Beth's campaign. It was a major improvement, if still a long way shy of the numbers Beth had proposed as targets. Three of the passes belonged to Mike. She didn't talk about it, or write anything in the newspaper, but, deep down, Beth was confident that she had had a hand in changing the lives of the students who had participated in the AP program, and gained the capabilities necessary to satisfy the examiner.

Something that she had not really anticipated had occurred. Although she had campaigned for the setting of system wide goals, it was in the elementary schools that she had proposed specific parental choice of program. She was not so naïve as to fail to recognize that her focus had fallen on the area of the schools where her own son was situated. But instead, what had actually happened, without any explicit recognition by the school district, was that choice in the form of AP classes had emerged in the High School. It was as if she had squeezed the balloon on one side, and a bulge had appeared on the other.

Absent system wide goals and a monitoring process, the trickle down effect that she had hoped would create a more rigorous curriculum in the middle school and elementary grades never really happened. Nobody ever victimized her children in school. In fact, quite the opposite. Staff all knew who she was, and who her children were, and went out of their way to make sure that nothing untoward happened to them. The last thing they wanted was to awaken the sleeping giant of Beth's activism. But the endless time-wasting poster projects never stopped. Each year, at least half of the days in school were spent reviewing material that had been covered in previous years.

The students who were prepared for the high school AP classes, and passed the exams, came from the families who cared enough to set high standards for themselves through the elementary and middle school years. They were arranging tutors, doing extra homework supervised by parents, and attending summer programs to supplement their knowledge and skills. But at least the AP classes existed where they had not before.

In the period following the election, several writers had delighted in branding Beth a "loser" in letters in the newspaper. Beth, though, had garnered an insight that perhaps only active participants in the political process ever fully understand. Politics is rarely so black and white as "winner" and "loser". A candidate may be defeated, but an idea, once introduced sufficiently compellingly, lives on beyond a single numerical verdict at the ballot box.

She had opened the eyes of her community to the concept that its public school system was not necessarily the omni-benevolent, highly effective organization that the propaganda trumpeted. Others had carried her campaign forward, not publicly or overtly, but through countless quiet discussions aimed at furthering the interests of their own families.

Long after her own psychological bruises and scrapes, incurred in the heat of a fierce political battle, had healed, the marks that she had inflicted on the organization of her school district remained. She reflected on that fact often, and with quiet satisfaction.

"Status quo, you know, that is Latin for 'the mess we're in.'"
Ronald Reagan, President of the United States

APRIL 2011

REYNOSA, MEXICO

The sun was going down in Reynosa but there was no "Miller time" for the endlessly turning machines. Outside the plant, cyclists, pedestrians, and the passengers recently disgorged from some rickety automobiles and buses crossed the dusty parking lot and began heading toward the door to begin the second shift. In a side room off the main shop floor, engineers huddled over sophisticated computer terminals refining the drawings of the next generation of more technically advanced products.

The company was developing a new plant that it planned to site in Asia. That night the technical drawings of both the new facility and the products that would be built there, each broken down into a string of digitized bits and bytes, would wing their way down a fiber optic cable under the Pacific Ocean. Every electronic pulse would carry with it a demand for future labor capacity that had once resided in the United States, was then transferred to Mexico, and would soon end up in India or China.

In a scene repeated across the continent, silently and invisibly the jobs that had once been the life blood of the United States middle class were being sucked away at the speed of light down thousands of microscopically thin glass tubes. All that remained was a gurgling sound, like a drinking straw on the last sip from a milk shake, and the burning question of where the refill would come from.

SUNBURY, NEW HAMPSHIRE

In Sunbury it was already almost dark. A car pulled up outside a large suburban house in a development of similar substantial abodes. There was something slightly less affluent, though, about the appearance of the neighborhood recently. Several of the properties looked as if the siding needed painting. Here and there, roof shingles were a little the worse for wear, and patches of mold were appearing. Amongst the small forest of for sale signs, several stood in yards that had clearly not been tended since the previous year, exhibiting symptoms of abandonment.

The driver didn't bother to get out, but sounded the horn in two prolonged bursts. Inside, two seventeen year old youths laid down video game handsets and hauled themselves off the couch they had occupied since returning from school three hours earlier. Not for them the strenuous homework effort needed to position themselves in the AP classes that were just beginning to emerge at the High School. "Cool" kids all pronounced AP to be seriously "lame" anyway.

"That'll be Jimmy. Hey, dude, make sure you, like, save that effing game, I'm creaming you, man."

"No way, man."

A middle aged woman appeared in the doorway.

"Where are you two off to tonight?"

"Watch a basketball game at Joey's, then a group of us are going to the mall to eat. We may be back late. Hey, Mom, I may just, like, skip school tomorrow. I need, like, a mental health day to catch up on my rest."

"Okay, honey, if that's what you think is best."

REYNOSA, MEXICO

South of the border, the machines kept turning, into the night.

Made in the USA
Middletown, DE
21 November 2016